# To Arms! To Arms, in Dixie!

### J. T. EDSON

A DELL BOOK

*For Richard and David of Replica Models (UK) Ltd.,
whose Winchesters, Colts, Thompsons, and Smith &
Wessons, and not forgetting the Remington Double
Derringers, have won many a gun battle for me.*

Published by
Dell Publishing
a division of
Bantam Doubleday Dell Publishing Group, Inc.
1540 Broadway
New York, New York 10036

ISBN: 0-440-21043-7

Printed in the United States of America

Published simultaneously in Canada

June 1993

10  9  8  7  6  5  4  3  2  1

RAD

# "BEHIND YOU, MASSA JIM!"
# WILLIE YELLED

Watching Bludso, Belle had not troubled to keep Tyrone under observation. Swinging her gaze in the mate's direction, she decided that Willie's warning was well founded.

Shaking his head from side to side, Tyrone was in a crouching position like a sprinter waiting to start a race. However, his right hand was less innocently occupied. It was reaching toward the quirt which he had earlier discarded.

From what Belle saw, the quirt served a second, more deadly purpose than as a mere inducer of recalcitrant horses. The force of its landing had caused the cap of the handle to separate from the remainder. Attached to the cap, and normally concealed inside the quirt, was a razor-sharp knife's blade.

*Books by J. T. Edson*

THE NIGHTHAWK
NO FINGER ON THE TRIGGER
THE BAD BUNCH
SLIP GUN
TROUBLED RANGE
THE FASTEST GUN IN TEXAS
THE HIDE AND TALLOW MEN
THE JUSTICE OF COMPANY Z
MCGRAW'S INHERITANCE
RAPIDO CLINT
COMANCHE
A MATTER OF HONOR
RENEGADE
WACO RIDES IN
BLOODY BORDER
ALVIN FOG, TEXAS RANGER
HELL IN THE PALO DURO
OLE DEVIL AT SAN JACINTO
GO BACK TO HELL
OLE DEVIL AND THE MULE TRAIN
VIRIDIAN'S TRAIL
OLE DEVIL AND THE CAPLOCKS

# To Arms! To Arms, in Dixie!

Author's note: *In answer to numerous requests I have received, here are the words which General Albert Pike, C.S.A., put to Daniel D. Emmet's minstrel song "Dixie."*

Southrons, hear your country call you,
Up, lest worse than death befall you,
To arms! To arms! To arms, in Dixie!
See the beacon fires are lighted,
Let Southron hearts now be united,
To arms! To arms! To arms, in Dixie!

*Chorus:*

Advance the flag of Dixie! Hurrah! Hurrah!
For Dixie's land we take our stand and live or die
    for Dixie,
To arms! To arms! We'll fight the world for Dixie!
To arms! To arms! We'll fight or die for Dixie!

Hear the Northern thunders mutter,
Yankee flags in South winds flutter,
To arms! *etc.*
Send them back your fierce defiance,

Stamp on that accursed alliance,
To arms! *etc.*

*Chorus:*

Fear no danger, shun no labor,
Take up rifle, pistol, sabre,
To arms! *etc.*
Shoulder pressing close to shoulder,
Let the odds make each heart bolder,
To arms! *etc.*

*Chorus:*

How the Southland's heart rejoices,
To the sound of loyal voices,
To arms! *etc.*
For faith betrayed and pledges broken,
Wrongs inflicted, insults spoken,
To arms! *etc.*

*Chorus:*

Strong as lions, swift as eagles,
Back to their kennels chase those beagles,
To arms! *etc.*
Cut the unequal bonds asunder,
Let Yankees hence each other plunder,
To arms! *etc.*

*Chorus:*

Swear upon the Southland's altar,
Never to submit or falter,
To arms! *etc.*

Until the Lord's work is completed,
And the spoilers are defeated,
To arms! To arms! To arms, in Dixie!

*Chorus:*

# 1
# THIS IS RECONSTRUCTION!

Raising his open, empty right hand, with its palm turned forward, high above his white-turbaned head, Sabot the Mysterious paused in an impressively dramatic manner. From the orchestra's pit, a deep, continuous rolling of the drums gave a warning that something special—possibly even the high spot of the evening's entertainment—was about to happen.

Clearly the audience deduced the required message from Sabot's attitude and the sound of the drums. Although his assistant—a beautiful, voluptuous brunette who wore the type of flimsy, revealing garments expected of a girl who had been "rescued from a life of sin in the Sultan of Tripoli's harem"—and a committee comprised of three men and an elderly woman shared the stage with him, the magician alone held the watchers' attention. Which was, of course, how it should be.

Stocky, of medium height, Sabot's sallow face sported spike-tipped mustachios and a sharp-pointed chin beard which combined to suggest foreign birth and upbringing. Nor did his Occidental black evening suit, frilly bosomed white silk shirt, and flowing scarlet silk cravat lessen the impression of the mysterious Orient created by his features and jewel-emblazoned turban.

Pausing to permit his audience's anticipation to build even higher, Sabot found himself pondering upon the possible cause of the vague, uneasy sensation that was eating at him. Something was wrong and, try as he might, he could not decide what it was.

Of course, even such an experienced performer as the magician might have been excused if he should feel perturbed under the prevailing conditions. Yet Sabot felt sure that his lack of ease was stemming out of another, more subtly disturbing influence. Unless he missed his guess, the cause of his concern had evolved out of something he had seen—or failed to see properly—since coming onto the stage. It did not, he believed, come from the wings or down in the well-filled auditorium.

That meant the sensation had its source in the committee, if indeed it existed at all.

Instinctively, if covertly, Sabot was watching the committee to make sure that their attention stayed on him and did not wander to the wings, where they might see something that should remain unobserved until the correct moment. He failed to detect any hint of what might be disturbing him. The three men were of the type who could be expected to come out of any audience. Prosperous-looking town dwellers, they were clearly enjoying their active participation in the show and the proximity of the scantily attired Princess Selima Baba. Nothing about such a commonplace trio could be responsible for his uneasy sensation, of that he felt certain.

Which left the woman as a possible suspect; and she appeared to be an even less likely candidate than the men. Tall, or she had been before age had bent her shoulders, and slenderly built, she had a face that was heavily powdered in a not too successful attempt to conceal its lines and wrinkles. For all that, in its day it could have been very beautiful. Drawn back in a tight bun, her dry, lifeless-looking gray hair supported an ancient, curly-brimmed, flower-decorated black hat. She wore a shapeless, stiff dark gray

Balmoral skirt that had been designed for a more bulky
figure. Its matching paletot coat had long sleeves and was
buttoned from the neck downward like a military tunic.
Black lace mitts covered sufficient of her hands and fingers
to prevent her marital status from being revealed. She
gripped an ancient vanity bag in both hands, nursing it
protectively on her lap. Earlier, in the course of a trick,
Sabot had produced a watch belonging to one of the male
members of the committee from her bag and had seen all
its meagre contents. Since then, she had sat clutching it
tightly as if she feared that other, more incriminating items
might be plucked from it.

Sabot allowed his gaze to linger briefly upon the woman.
Going by her appearance, it seemed strange that she
should have consented to come onto the stage. There was
an air of faded gentility and respectability about her which
hinted that she had known better, more affluent days, yet
did not lend itself to exhibitionist tendencies. Her kind
usually shied well away from actions which might be con-
strued as making a public display of themselves. Yet she
had been one of the first to rise when Sabot had made his
usual request for a committee to scrutinize his tricks at
close quarters and try to explain away how each was performed.

Diverting his glance, Sabot darted a scowl at his assistant. Although shapely and visually attractive in her
"harem" costume, Selima left a lot to be desired in the way
she performed her duties. A more astute member of the
act would have evaded the woman's offer to join the committee, especially under the circumstances. Even in normal
conditions, such a person would not have been a good
choice. Knowing the woman's type, the audience might believe that she was a shill in his employ and not a genuine
patron of the performance. However, he consoled himself,
his present audience should have small cause for complaint
even if she had been a shill.

The Grand Palace Theater at Shreveport, Louisiana, was

packed to capacity that night. Its patrons formed much the same general cross section of the population as had attended the other performances during Sabot's ten-day engagement. Being a major stopping point on the Red River, drawing custom and profit from the north- and southbound traffic, the town had thrown off most of the poverty left in the wake of the War Between the States. Sufficiently so for theatergoing to have returned, as a regular diversion, to a level where it was profitable for performers of Sabot's standing and importance to include the Grand Palace in their itineraries.

Not that tonight's show would be profitable in a monetary sense. Out of gratitude for the excellent attendances during his stay, Sabot had offered to donate one final appearance—before moving north to Mooringsport on the riverboat *Texarkana Belle* at midnight and commencing a tour of Texas's towns—without charge to all such members of the late Confederate States Army and Navy as might care to attend.

In view of the local situation with regard to the United States Army, especially that section of it based on the outskirts of town, the offer might have been considered—to say the least—tactless and ill-advised. However, the camp's commanding officer, Lieutenant Colonel Szigo—a bitter, disappointed man whose dislike of the South and Southrons showed in his clinging to the outmoded title of garrison—had had no cause for complaint over the magician's apparent discrimination. On the night after his arrival in Shreveport, Sabot had donated an equally profitless performance for the men under Szigo's command.

Such apparent favoritism might have cost Sabot dearly by alienating him from the civilian population of Shreveport, who had had little reason to hold friendly feelings for the soldiers. That it had not was a tribute to his smooth talking and knowledge of human nature. In a statement to the *Shreveport Herald-Times* concerning his generosity to the "Yankees," he had pointed out that the War ended back in 'Sixty-Five and how many a gallant ex-Rebel now wore the blue uniform of the United States Army. That might have had little effect in a town where the senior Army officer insisted on speaking of his command as a "garrison," with all its connotations of the recently ended Reconstruction period. However, Sabot had gone on to declare that he believed the citizens of Shreveport were sufficiently fair- and open-minded not to hold the soldiers' free performance against him. In a less enlightened and forward-looking community, he had continued, he would not have dared to make such a gesture, but felt certain that he could do so in Shreveport.

Faced with such a comment, the citizens' civic pride had compelled them to lay aside any objections they might have wished to express. Some of the more responsible members of the community had even hoped that, as a result of the free shows, a better and more friendly relationship with the Army might be forthcoming.

Certainly Colonel Szigo had shown an eagerness to improve matters which he had not previously displayed. Despite the general consensus of public opinion, he had raised no objections to the show for the ex-Rebels. In fact, he had even gone so far as to make what amounted to a gesture of good will. To ensure that there would be no incidents or open clashes between his soldiers and the local population—which had been an all-too-regular occurrence in the past—he had placed the whole town off limits to all military personnel on the evening of the civilians' free performance.

How much of that sensible decision had been influenced by Sabot, only Colonel Szigo and the magician could have said. Throughout his show's stay in Shreveport Sabot had worked hard to win the confidence of the Army's officers and the town's leading, most respected citizens. Judging by Szigo's response—and the presence of those same citizens in the audience—he had met with some success in his endeavors.

The rolling of the drums ended without Sabot having reached any conclusion as to why he was experiencing the uneasy sensation. In the breathless hush that followed, Selima undulated her way to the garishly colored and decorated prop box. From it, she lifted an inflated red balloon. Exhibiting the balloon prominently to the audience, she tossed it into the air.

Rotating his raised wrist, so that he displayed both sides of it, Sabot plucked a shining, nickel-plated Remington Double Derringer apparently out of thin air. All in the same motion, he aimed upwards and fired. Hit by the charge of minute birdshot, with which he had replaced the usual solid lead ball of the pistol's .41 rimfire cartridge, the balloon disintegrated in a violent puff of bright red smoke.

At which point, before the sense of anticlimax could start to creep home on the audience, the evening's previously harmless, enjoyable entertainment began to take on a very serious, even alarming, note.

Coinciding with the explosion of the balloon, four large portraits unrolled from where they had been suspended, concealed by the upper fringes of the stage's decorative curtaining. The sight of them, or rather a realization of the subjects which they represented, brought a startled, concerted gasp from the people seated at the various tables in the auditorium.

The first portrait on the right depicted a background of burning houses and crops stretching off toward the horizon. In the foreground was an excellent likeness of the Federal Army's General William Tecumseh Sherman, wearing a dark blue dress uniform and holding a flaming torch. In a speech balloon, he was ordering his brutal and clearly delighted soldiers to "Loot and burn all you want, men. I'll see that you're not punished for it."

Having as its background the sidewalk outside the First National Bank of New Orleans, the front of which was clearly named, the second painting showed the Union's

General Benjamin F. Butler emerging from the broken-open main entrance. Grasping a large sack labeled "Bank Deposits," he was exhorting villainously featured Yankee enlisted men—who were engaged in tearing the clothes from a well-dressed, terrified woman and two young girls—to "Go to it, men. Treat all their women like common whores!"

On the third poster, in front of scenes of Union soldiers torturing Confederate prisoners, General Smethurst gloatingly supervised the crew of a Gatling gun as they fired at a group of bound and gagged victims in one of the prisoner-of-war camps which he had commanded. He was complaining, "I wish I had more of these Secessionist scum to test the gun on."

The final portrait was more recent in its text. Topped by a large printed message in glaring red ink which read "THIS IS RECONSTRUCTION!" it illustrated a mob of drunken Negroes wrecking and looting a general store. In the foreground, a burly, vicious-looking blue-clad sergeant was using the butt of his rifle to club down the white civilian owner of the store and warning, "You aren't allowed to stop them robbing you, Johnny Reb, they're black!"

If the subject matter of the four paintings had been intended as a joke, it fell remarkably flat. More than that; in view of the local situation with regard to the Army, the paintings might be considered more than tactless reminders of the past and could be dangerous. However, the surprises of the evening had not ended.

Almost before the portraits had completely unrolled from their places of concealment, a figure grasping a twin-barreled, ten-gauge sawed-off shotgun appeared at each of the four exits. They wore plain-colored, almost nondescript suits devoid of any identifying features. The desire for anonymity was carried even further. Each of them wore a black mask, suspended from the brim of his hat to below the level of his chin, which effectively concealed his face.

From their positions on the stage, the members of the

committee were unable to see the fronts of the portraits. They could, however, tell by the reactions of the audience and the appearance of the masked men that something far out of the ordinary was happening. Then they had further cause for alarm, and much closer to hand.

Three more masked men walked from the left-side wings. Only one, the bulkiest if not tallest, was openly armed. He too carried a sawed-off shotgun. By his clothing, which matched that of the watchers at the exits, he was of inferior social standing to his empty-handed companions. One of them was taller than the armed man, although slighter in build. The other was something over medium height, well-made, and carried himself with a brash, straight-backed swagger seen mainly among arrogant, rank-conscious Army officers. Their attire was that of wealthy gentlemen attending an informal, yet important, social gathering with their equals.

Showing symptoms of alarm, the three male members of the committee rose hurriedly from their chairs. The woman also came to her feet, moving with considerable speed for one of her age. Darting a glance toward the intruders as they approached, she made as if to move toward the front of the stage.

"No sudden moves, fellers!" warned the bulkiest of the trio, gesturing with his shotgun and employing a tone in keeping with his clothing. "Just sit down a spell and nobody'll get hurt."

From his perplexed expression, Sabot had been completely taken aback by the unexpected turn of events. His whole being left an impression that he had no idea what was going on. Then the burly man's growled-out words seemed to jolt him out of his state of shock and arouse an instinct to protest. Bracing back his shoulders, he stalked grimly toward the masked intruders.

"How dare you come in here," the magician demanded, bristling with righteous indignation, "interrupting my perform—"

Striding by his better-dressed companions, the burly man snapped around his shotgun with casual-seeming, yet trained precision. Its butt thudded against the side of Sabot's jaw and knocked him staggering to sprawl onto the floor at the rear of the stage. As the magician collapsed in a huddled heap upon his hands and knees, a rumble of protest rose from the audience. Immediately, the men at the exits elevated their weapons to a greater position of readiness. It seemed likely that the people in the auditorium would rush the intruders and avenge their benefactor.

"That's for you, you Yankee-loving son of a bitch!" bellowed Sabot's assailant, in a voice that carried above the protests of the audience. "Anybody foot-licks to the blue-bellies like you do deserves anything he gets from a loyal Southron."

Backed by the very real, deadly menace of the shotguns at the exits, the man's statement served to quieten down the expressions of disapproval. His words recalled certain feelings many of the audience had harbored concerning Sabot's friendship with the disliked blue-bellies. Remembering, they were less inclined to take active measures to avenge his injuries. Especially when doing so might result in death or injury for many of themselves. At least, they would not make the attempt without another, stronger and more personal reason for doing it.

Inadvertently, the female member of the committee suggested just such a reason.

"Wha-what do you want?" she shrilled, clutching even tighter at her vanity bag and displaying far greater alarm or concern than Princess Selima Baba was showing. "If this is a robbery—"

Again the menacing rumblings crept through the audience. Men who would have hesitated to take action on behalf of a "Yankee-lover" were prepared to be defiant in defence of their property.

# 2

# YOU WON'T STOP ME
# LEAVING

Clearly the taller of the unarmed intruders on the stage did not underestimate the potential danger to his party that had been caused by the elderly woman's suggestion. The mask he wore concealed whatever expression might be on his face, but his whole attitude was one of quiet reassurance as he swung in her direction.

"Calm yourself, ma'am," the man requested politely. His voice was that of a well-educated Southern gentleman. "I assure you that we have not come here to commit a robbery." Turning from the woman, he faced the audience and raised his arms in a signal for silence. "Please remain seated, ladies and gentlemen. There is no cause for alarm. You have my word that we mean no harm to any of you."

Such was the apparent honesty in the man's tone that the audience started to relax once more. Even the most unthinking of them realized that outlaws would hardly go to so much trouble to commit a crime that would yield only small returns. The loot that they might hope to gather would hardly justify the risks.

To strengthen the point made by their spokesman, the watchers at the exits relaxed. The shotguns sank to point at the floor, implying that their wielders no longer felt a need to remain vigilant. Natural curiosity caused the men and women at the tables to settle down and await further developments.

"You there, shameless foreign woman!" barked the second of the weaponless newcomers, in a hard, commanding voice that had traces of a well-educated Southern accent. "Go over and attend to your master."

"Sure thing, mister," Selima answered, with a remarkably American-sounding voice considering that she had been "rescued from a life of sin in the Sultan of Tripoli's harem." "Anything you say."

Crossing the stage with the same sensually jaunty, hip-rolling gait that had graced all her movements—drawing numerous lascivious glances from the men on the committee and causing the elderly woman to deliver almost as many disapproving glares—the girl halted and bent over her employer. She did this in a manner which prominently displayed the full curvaceous quality of her buttocks under their flimsy pantaloons. Nothing in her posture and behavior implied that she harbored fears for her own safety or concern over her employer's possible injuries. Rather she comported herself with the air of one who was playing a well-rehearsed scene from a melodrama—but was playing it remarkably badly.

Watching the way in which Selima carried out his companion's order, the taller of the unarmed pair made a gesture that might have indicated annoyance. It almost appeared, to at least one observer, that he took exception to the brunette's too casual acceptance of what should have been an alarming and unprecedented sequence of events. However, he made no comment on the matter. Instead, he returned his attention to the restlessly moving audience.

"Ladies and gentlemen!" the tall man boomed out, his words reaching every corner of the auditorium. "You are all probably wondering why my companions and I have seen fit to intrude upon your evening's entertainment in such a manner. This charming lady"—he indicated the elderly woman as she sat staring intently at him and bowed slightly in her direction—"suggested that we might be contemplating a robbery. That is not so. Instead of taking from you, we hope that we may be able to help you regain something that we have all lost. We want to give you back your —FREEDOM!"

An excited, yet also disturbed rustle of conversation arose among the audience, swelling louder in the dramatic pause which followed the speaker's final shouted word. Most of Sabot's guests were aware that, taken with the four dangling portraits, the speech they had heard carried serious, dangerous implications. The civil law enforcement authorities and, more particularly, the local Army commander might easily call it treason.

Despite their understanding, the men in the audience hesitated. As usual in times of stress, or when faced with a situation completely out of the ordinary, the majority were waiting for guidance on how to act. They were also hoping that somebody else in their number would accept the responsibility of becoming their leader.

Aware of how a crowd's mentality worked, the spokesman of the intruders scanned the auditorium. He saw a figure stand up at the table reserved for the most important members of the audience.

"You have a question, sir?" the masked man inquired amiably, pointing in the other's direction.

"No, sir," replied the man from the audience. "I intend to leave."

Instantly every eye focused upon the speaker. Tall, slim, in his early fifties, he was dressed fashionably and in perfect taste. His whole appearance hinted at military training and self-confidence. Most of the audience recognized him as Colonel Alburgh Winslow, attorney-at-law, a member of the Louisiana State Legislature and owner of the *Shreveport Herald-Times*. Well-liked, respected as a pillar of the community, the people in the auditorium figured that his lead in the affair would be worth following.

So the rest of the audience sat back and waited to see

what the masked men's response would be. And, more important, to discover how Colonel Winslow would react if his intention of leaving should be opposed.

"You served in the Army of the Confederate States, sir?" asked the spokesman of the intruders, in flat, impersonal, but neither threatening nor angry tones.

"I had the honor to command the 6th Louisiana Rifles under General Braxton Bragg, sir," Winslow answered, returning politeness with civility. "But I have also taken the oath of allegiance to the Union—"

"That was your right, sir," the spokesman conceded courteously. "Most of us present took it in good faith and the belief that the Yankees would honor their side of it."

"They sure as hell didn't do that!" bawled a male voice from the rear of the auditorium, and a mumble of concurrence rose from his area.

"You are free to leave, sir, if you so wish it," the masked spokesman stated, when the hubbub had died away. "All I ask is that you will give me your word as a Southern gentleman that you will not speak of what is happening here before tomorrow morning at the earliest."

"You won't stop me leaving if I do?" Winslow asked.

"Your word will be sufficient guarantee for us, sir," replied the spokesman. "We've no intention of stopping *anybody* leaving. All we need from those who go is an assurance that they will do nothing to prevent the rest of us from continuing with this meeting."

There was a shuffling of feet, but still nobody showed any inclination of accepting the offer to depart. They were still awaiting Winslow's lead.

"I'll go further," the shorter of the unarmed intruders went on, drawing the elderly woman's gaze to him until she seemed to be hanging on his every word. Through the slits in his mask, his eyes raked the six prominent citizens who shared Winslow's table. "We, *all* of us in this room, would prefer those who aren't loyal to the South to leave immediately."

"Let the gentleman pass there," the spokesman ordered the guard nearest to Winslow. "Let anybody pass who wants to go."

"Thank you, sir," Winslow drawled, after a moment's thought. "I'll stay and hear you out."

Taken with the second man's comment on loyalty to the South, Winslow's refusal to accept the offer to depart brought to an end the muttering among the other patrons who had intended to leave. They were mostly businessmen who had regained some measure of their prosperity after being impoverished by the War. Some drew an appreciable amount of their business from the Army, so had no desire to take a part in what Colonel Szigo would certainly regard as a treasonable assembly. On the other hand, they had no wish to label themselves as disloyal to the Southern States. That could be just as damaging, perhaps even more so, to their local business prospects. So they concluded that they would accept Winslow's guidance and remain. Later, if necessary, they could disclaim any association with the sentiments expressed by the intruders.

Assisted by Selima, Sabot the Mysterious dragged himself erect. Leaning on the girl's shoulder, with a trickle of blood running from the corner of his mouth, he scowled at his assailant. Jerking a thumb contemptuously in the magician's direction, the spokesman instructed his armed companion to remove the Yankee-loving trash and attend to his injury. Going over, the burly man herded Selima and Sabot into the wings and beyond the audience's range of vision. The couple went without protest. Any concern the guests might have felt was lessened by the reminder of Sabot's "Yankee-loving" tendencies and the thought that his hurts would receive attention.

"Ma'am, gentlemen," the masked spokesman said, drawing the elderly woman's gaze from the departing magician, girl, and their escort. "Perhaps you would oblige me by returning to your seats in the auditorium?"

"We sure will, mister," confirmed one of the male members of the committee, rising with alacrity.

Sharing their companion's desire to be disassociated from the masked intruders, the other two men showed an equal haste to quit the stage. Although she flashed another quick look at where Sabot's party had disappeared into the wings, the elderly woman wasted no time in following the three citizens.

With the stage cleared of all but himself and his smaller companion, the tall, imposing masked figure commenced a carefully thought-out and excellently delivered speech. He started by reminding the audience that, from the earliest days of its conception, the United States had agreed upon one certain matter of policy. If any State should feel that its policies and domestic arrangements were not in keeping with the remainder, or that the Federal Government's decisions were against its best interests, it had the inalienable right to secede, withdraw, from the Union.

"This is the *right* that the people up North refused to grant us," the man went on, his voice throbbing with emotion. "They begrudged us our heritage, envied our way of life and culture. But they wanted to keep right on digging their grasping Yankee hands into our pockets. They didn't want the Southern States, but they *did* want the money which was wrung from us in taxes. And that, ladies and gentlemen, is why those noble Abolitionists up North fought to retain the Union."

Going by the growl which sounded from the main body of the hall, there was considerable agreement with the man's words. At the table holding the important members of the community, more than one pair of eyes darted worried glances at Winslow. Giving a quick shake of his head in reply to the unasked questions, he flickered a look toward the elderly woman. She sat at a lower-priced table, subjecting both the masked men on the stage to a careful scrutiny and listening intently to the response to the speech.

Covering the South's original victories, the speaker touched briefly upon the behind-the-scenes reasons why the first thrust of successes had not been exploited to the full. He also intimated that, in the event of another clash with the Yankees, there would be no such loss of advantage. Then he praised the gallantry, courage, and loyalty of the Confederate States Army and Navy as they had battled against a numerically, industrially, and economically superior enemy.

"They might have had better arms, food, and supplies," he stated proudly, "but, by the Lord, they didn't have better *men!*"

"And this time we won't be fighting them alone," the second man announced, after the thunder of applause which had greeted the other's declaration had ebbed away. "Our friends in Europe are willing to send arms, equipment, supplies to help us fight the Northern oppressors."

"Which friends in Europe?" Winslow challenged.

"We can't mention the country, for obvious reasons," the spokesman answered. "But I give you my word as a Southern gentleman that a powerful European country is prepared to back us in our fight for freedom."

"For what price, sir?" Winslow demanded.

"That will be decided between our two Governments," the spokesman replied, hiding any displeasure he might be feeling at the questions. He pointed to the first portrait on the right, continuing, "You may ask why we should need the aid of a foreign country. There is the answer. That is how the Yankees make war. Not against soldiers, but against the harmless, defenseless civilian population."

Without giving Winslow an opportunity to extend the questioning about the identity of the European country that was willing to ally itself with the Confederate cause, the spokesman enlarged upon the horrors of Sherman's "march to the sea."

Winslow realized that he was being frozen out, but did not try to force the issue. To do so might swing the crowd even further in the masked intruders' favor. Its more impressionable members would recollect that the spokesman was willing to take Winslow's word as a Southern gentleman on the matter of keeping silent after he had been allowed to depart. So the Colonel ought to return the compliment by accepting the spokesman's assurance—backed by his word—that the European ally existed.

Deftly the spokesman drew a lurid picture of how Sherman had implemented a policy of wholesale arson during "the march." Not content with the hardships that had been caused to the civilian population, he had given his oral and written assurance that no man under his command would be placed on trial or punished in any way for looting.

"And so, my friends," the spokesman continued, "whole families were stripped bare of their possessions and left destitute, while Yankee officers and enlisted men amassed fortunes under those damnable orders which gave them the right to loot and pillage with impunity. Yet, debased as they were, Sherman's marauders did not sink to the depths of Butler or Smethurst."

There would be few in the audience to argue against *that* point.

Enlarging upon the former officer, the spokesman told of how he had "acquired" and converted to his own use some eight hundred thousand dollars held in the Dutch Consul's office in New Orleans. Probably, the masked man went on, he had further increased his fortune by other, undisclosed thefts. Certainly he had permitted his soldiers to go even further in their excesses than Sherman had allowed and to do worse than burn or loot. Butler's most notorious order—which, although the man omitted to mention the fact, General U. S. Grant had rescinded as soon as it had come to his attention—had read, *"If any woman give insult or offense to an officer or soldier of the Union Army, she shall be regarded and held liable to be treated as a woman of the streets plying her avocation."* According to the spokesman, Butler's troops had eagerly grasped the opportunities offered by such a vicious, ill-advised command decision.

Since the end of the War, Butler had allied himself with the most radical section of the Republican Party. He was notorious for his inflammatory speeches advocating strict controls and restrictions being retained on the Southern States—which did little to make ex-Rebels forget his iniquities in New Orleans. Butler's behavior made an even more telling point than Sherman's, for the latter had proven a humane and moderate man in peace.

Although Smethurst's command of the Union's prisoner-of-war camps had been notorious, with stories of deliberate starvation, wanton brutality, vicious torture, and general mistreatment of the captives. Winslow felt that he was a weak link in the intruders' arguments. There had been rumors of prisoners being used to test experimental weapons—hotly denied in the North, but firmly believed below the Mason-Dixon line—but he had been killed in Texas after the War had ended.* So, while the memory of his misdeeds remained, the crowd would be less inclined to hate Yankees in general on his account.

The speaker pointed out that conditions had undoubtedly been bad in the South's Andersonville prisoner-of-war camp, but explained that there had been mitigating circumstances. Due to the United States Navy's piracy and blockade on Confederate ports, food and medical supplies had been in short supply all through the South. While the camp's staff had done their best, obviously the prisoners had had to take second place to Southron needs. In the event of a further confrontation, the undisclosed European country would ensure that similar shortages did not occur.

Much as Winslow would have liked to make a further investigation into the identity of the European ally, he was denied the opportunity. Launching straight into the subject

* *Why and how Smethurst was killed is told in* The Hooded Riders.

of the last poster, the spokesman was on firmer, more familiar ground.

Vividly the spokesman cataloged the abuses and injustices perpetrated by Union officials and carpetbagger politicians who had been sent to administer the beaten Southern States. In this he was helped by the fact that the kind of situation illustrated on the portrait had been very close to the actions and sentiments of the North's occupying Armies during the early days of Reconstruction. Memories were still fresh of Negro "committees" set up to govern communities; many of which had been comprised of a drunken rabble intent on defiling or destroying everything white, knowing that the Army's bayonets would back them up no matter how bad their actions.

In Winslow's opinion, the spokesman had just made his best argument. The behavior of the soldiers under Szigo's command had served to keep alive the resentments of Reconstruction.

"And, my friends, that is what Yankee 'fair dealing' and Reconstruction has meant—nay! still is meaning to the South!" the masked man thundered. "For too long we have been held in bondage by the grasping Yankees. You have all witnessed and suffered from the arrogance of the garrison in your town. Do you wish to continue living under its heels?"

If the thunderous response from the cheaper tables at the rear was anything to go by, at least one section of the audience had no wish for the prevailing situation to continue. To give them their due, the occupants of the lower-priced tables were the citizens who had seen and suffered most from the worst aspects of the soldiers' behavior. It was at their saloons or entertainments that the antipathy had flared many times into open conflict. So there was little love lost between the blue-clad troops and the people who saw them at their worst. Especially as the commanding officer had never seen fit to give compensation to those who had suffered financial losses through his men's bad conduct, nor to control and punish the offenders.

"May I ask, sir," Winslow boomed, springing to his feet in an attempt to prevent the intruder from stirring up even greater ill-feeling against the soldiers, "why you have come here tonight?"

"Because the day of reckoning is at hand for the Yankees," the spokesman replied. "The time for striking back is drawing near."

"You mean for us once again to secede from the Union?"

"That, sir, is exactly what I mean!"

"Are we ready for such an extreme step?" Winslow inquired, hoping to sow the seeds of doubt among the audience. "It would mean open war with the North."

"We didn't flinch from *that* before," the spokesman pointed out.

"But we were prepared—" Winslow began, meaning to point out that the South had been in a condition of readiness for war which no longer existed.

"And we're prepared to fight again!" the man interrupted. "We were willing to continue the fight in 'Sixty-Five, but our leaders made peace. No, gentlemen, I don't blame General Lee for doing so. He acted, according to his belief, for the best and according to his orders from our Government. They were men of honor, deluded by the belief that they were dealing with honorable men. So they stopped the fighting, accepting honorable terms. But did the Yankees keep to their end of the bargain?"

"Like hell they did!" roared a voice from the rear, and rousing cheers echoed the sentiment.

"As our friend says, like hell they did!" the spokesman shouted. "So, I say to you, we Southrons are no longer bound by the Yankees' dishonored allegiance. The time is coming when the South will rise again. To arms! To arms, in Dixie!"

As if in answer to the clarion call of the man's final

words, a large Stars and Bars flag of the Confederate
States unfurled—apparently of its own volition—at the
back of the stage. Raising his baton, the conductor of the
attenuated orchestra—Sabot's charity had not extended to
paying the theater's regular staff of musicians, and he had
been making do with only his own four men—gave a signal. The familiar strains of a tune rose from the orchestra
pit. It was "Dixie," long since adopted as the anthem of the
Confederate States.

Snapping smartly to attention, the two masked men on
the stage began to sing General Albert Pike's fiercely patri-
otic words to what Daniel D. Emmet had originally com-
posed as a cheerful, innocent minstrel song. Wood scraped
on wood as man after man stood up. Slowly, yet with an
ever-increasing volume, the singing spread through the
hall.

> *Southrons, hear your country call you!*
> *Up, lest worse than death befall you!*
> *To arms! To arms! To arms, in Dixie!*
> *See the beacon fires are lighted!*
> *Let Southron hearts now be united!*
> *To arms! To arms! To arms, in Dixie!*

Standing as straight and proud as any member of the
audience, Winslow added his voice to those of the others.
His eyes met those of the elderly woman who had been
part of Sabot's committee, and he could read the deep
concern and worry on her face.

# 3
# TELL THE FRENCHMAN
# ABOUT IT

"Well, Alburgh," said the plump, perspiring president of the Shreveport Rivermen's Bank as their party left the theater, "what do we do now?"

"We gave our words in there that we wouldn't do anything before tomorrow morning," Cullinan, owner of the town's biggest livery barn, grain, and fodder store, pointed out.

"That we did," agreed a third, equally prominent member of the party. "And, let us not forget, they've taken Sabot's girl along with them as a hostage against his good behavior. If we should set the law on to them, they might think he'd done it and harm her."

"Would they go that far?" the bank's president inquired. "The two on the stage sounded like gentlemen."

"And both know what they can expect from the Yankees if they're caught after tonight," Cullinan answered. "Are *we* prepared to take the chance that they *won't* harm her?"

"Well, *I* for one don't intend on going back on *my* word," declared another of the party. "I gave it of my own free will and I'll keep it. So I'm going straight home and staying there."

"Szigo's going to be riled to hell when he hears about it and that we didn't go immediately to tell him what had happened," warned the president of the bank. "He might even claim that we were a party to it and will certainly say that we should have done something to prevent it happening."

"That's for sure," Cullinan agreed, sounding worried. A large proportion of his profits came from supplying the Army's needs. "The fact that we gave our words not to report the incident until morning won't carry any weight with him."

"Szigo's no longer in command," Winslow remarked quietly.

"No longer in command?" Cullinan repeated. "I hadn't heard any mention of him being replaced."

"Nor had he," Winslow replied. "I want you to treat this as confidential, boys, although there'll be no great need after tomorrow. A friend of mine in Washington heard of Szigo's behavior and passed it on to the War Department. They're putting a new man in command. I met him this afternoon, before he went out to the camp. Take it from me, Colonel Manderley's not like Szigo."

"So what do we do, Alburgh?" Cullinan insisted.

"Here's Hector with my carriage now," Winslow answered, pointing along the street. "I'm going home. What I suggest is that you boys leave it with me."

"There's no great point in breaking our words, anyway," said the man who had insisted he would not. "That fifteen minutes' grace they had us grant them will have given them time to make good their escape."

"They're long gone already and will be well clear before the Army can start looking for them," Cullinan decided, sounding relieved at the other's support for his conclusions. "I'm all for doing as Alburgh says. There's nothing to be gained by going to the Army and making a fuss."

"That will only keep the affair in the public's eye," the president remarked. "We'd better to let it be forgotten. Who wants a ride home with me?"

"I'll come," Cullinan offered. "Let us know what this new colonel thinks about it, Alburgh."

"I'll do that," Winslow promised, and watched his party disintegrate as its members went to their waiting carriages.

"Could I trouble you for a ride, Colonel?" asked the elderly woman, crossing the sidewalk before Winslow could board his own vehicle. "A poor old body like me's not used to such exciting goings-on."

"It'll be a pleasure, ma'am," Winslow replied, doffing his hat gallantly. "Allow me to help you to enter."

If any of the excited, chattering crowd streaming from the theater noticed the woman addressing Winslow, they attached no significance to the sight. Their heads were too full of what they had witnessed in the building for them to think about what was perfectly natural behavior on Winslow's part. A Southron gentleman of the finest kind, he could be expected to render assistance if it was requested by a member of the opposite sex.

Slouching casually in the doorway of the cafe adjacent to the theater, two big, burly men paid greater attention to Winslow's activities. Bare-headed, with close-cropped hair, they had hard, clean-shaven, tanned features. Their long black civilian cloak-coats effectively concealed all their other garments except for highly polished, spur-decorated, Wellington-leg riding boots. Retaining their positions, they watched Winslow open the door of his carriage and help the woman climb in.

"Well, that's done," said the shorter of the pair, sounding pleased, as Winslow followed the woman.

"How'd you mean?" demanded his companion.

"We don't need to keep watching him. He didn't come out before the others. Now he's got that old gal with him, he'll not be going to the camp or the marshal's office."

"The Colonel said for us to follow him—" began the larger man.

"And stop him if he looked like he was going to fetch the law—" the other interrupted.

*"And* trail him home if he went there," the larger reminded the shorter coldly. "Then we wait for the other
boys to join us."

"Aw, Matt—"

"Don't forget, Winslow's the main one we're after,"
Matt growled, watching Winslow's carriage drive by. Its
curtains had been drawn across the windows and he could
not see inside. "Let's go."

Followed by his scowling companion, Matt went to
where a buggy stood in an alley. Taking the reins as he
climbed aboard, Matt started the horse and guided it after
Winslow's carriage.

If the hard-faced pair had been able to see into their
quarry's vehicle, they would have received a surprise. Letting out a long sigh of relief, the "elderly" woman straightened and flexed her "age-bent" shoulders.

"Whew! That's better," she said in a vibrant Southern
drawl far different from the tones she had used in the
theater. "Stooping that way's not the easiest thing to do for
any length of time."

"I don't suppose it is," Winslow answered, showing no
surprise at his passenger's remarkable change of voice.
"You did it very well."

Reaching up, the woman removed not only her hat but
her gray "hair" at the same time. Doing so exposed black
locks which had been cropped boyishly short to the contours of her skull. Producing a bandanna from her vanity
bag, she rubbed vigorously at her cheeks. The powder and
"age" lines departed, leaving behind a beautiful face that
showed intelligence and strength of will.

"I was getting worried that the magician had realized I
was disguised," she remarked at the completion of her
metamorphosis. "He kept glancing at me in a nervous
manner. This wig is good, but it's not the same as real
hair."

Unconsciously, the girl had struck upon the cause of Sabot's perturbation. He had noticed, in passing, a slight un-

reality in the "elderly woman's" hair and the memory of it had remained in the back of his mind but was unable to break through.

"What did you make of it, Uncle Alburgh?" the girl inquired.

"I didn't like any part of it," Winslow admitted.

"Most of the audience seemed to," the girl pointed out. "They cheered him loud and long when he finished speaking. And nobody offered to leave for the full fifteen minutes after he and his men had gone."

After the singing of "Dixie," the spokesman for the intruders had stated that the meeting had lasted as long as was safe for his party or the audience. Then he had taken precautions against the intruders' departure. First the magician had been returned to the stage. Sabot's face was no longer bleeding and he had declared that he was unharmed. However, his assistant was to be taken as a hostage by the masked men. If there had been no pursuit, they had undertaken to return her in time to catch the *Texarkana Belle*. Promising that he would behave, he had begged the audience not to do anything which might endanger Selima.

Next the spokesman had asked the audience—directing his words mainly to Winslow's party—that they should give their words not to inform the authorities until the following morning, by which time he and his men would be out of harm's way. Lastly, he had requested that the audience remain seated for fifteen minutes after his party had taken their departure. That would, he had assured them, give adequate opportunity for their escape.

"He was smart, without a doubt," Winslow observed. "Although he claimed they were only taking the girl to ensure Sabot's good behavior, he knew that we would hesitate to do anything that might endanger her. And we, my party, were those most likely to report the meeting to the authorities. Blast it, Belle, I should have followed my inclination and walked straight out."

"I'd say the men knew you," answered the girl. "Or read your character pretty well."

"I don't follow you."

"Anybody who *knows* you would realize that, without forcibly detaining you, they couldn't have made you stay against your will. And you're too popular for them to want to use force. So they offered to let you go, knowing they could trust your word if you promised not to report them."

"They could."

"So they were gambling on you being curious enough to stop, just so long as it was clear that nobody was trying to make you," the girl went on.

"Huh!" Winslow grunted, but made no further comment on the girl's assessment of his character and motives. "If I'd left, a lot would have followed."

"Not after the other man's speech about loyalty to the South," argued the girl. "And I feel sure that they'd made arrangements to deal with anybody who did try to leave. Tell Hector to stop, please."

"What's wrong?" Winslow asked, after he had complied with the request.

"A whole lot of things," the girl replied. "What was your impression of the man who did most of the talking?"

"He was well educated, shrewd, and as hard as nails. A gentleman by birth and upbringing," Winslow decided, after a moment's thought.

"Did he, or his companion, strike you as being French?" asked the girl.

When Winslow's carriage had come to a halt, Matt had been compelled to keep his vehicle moving. They were on a deserted stretch of street, and the buggy would have been too conspicuous if he had stopped. Warning his companion, whom he addressed as "Hermy," not to display interest in the carriage as they passed, he steered the horse to go by it. Continuing for about fifty yards, he found an intersection. Turning out of Hector's sight, he reined in the horse.

"Go keep watch from the corner," Matt growled.

"You're a mite free with your orders," Hermy protested sullenly. "Them three bars on your sleeve don't count for a heap on this chore."

"So tell the Frenchman about it," Matt sniffed. "Only make your will *afore* you do it. You won't get a chance *after* you've said your piece."

"Ain't he the mean bastard," Hermy remarked in a conciliatory manner, turning to lift a corner of the blanket which covered something behind their seat.

"Leave the hat there, blast it!" Matt snapped in exasperation, showing no sign of being mollified. "If somebody sees you wearing it, they could come and start asking questions."

Removing his hand, Hermy climbed from the buggy. He swaggered away as if keeping the carriage under observation had been his own idea. The cloak-coat trailed open as he walked, exposing his legs. The dark blue riding breeches which showed had a yellow stripe along the outside of each thigh.

"No," Winslow declared, after considering the girl's question, "I don't think either of them was French."

"Did you recognize either of them? I mean, did they seem familiar?"

"Not that I could put a finger on it. And I know all the men of their class in Caddo and Bossier Counties. Do you know something about them?"

"Not much," the girl answered. "I've heard a little about their activities."

"Do you mean that they've done this kind of thing before?"

"Nothing so blatant and open. But I was told that Shreveport would be different from the other meetings which have been held throughout the South."

"How did you become involved, Belle?" Winslow inquired.

"I'm a member of the United States Secret Service," the

girl explained, sounding just a mite defensive and challenging.

"Dad-blast it, Belle!" Winslow barked, showing no great surprise at her answer. "I never took to the notion of you and Cousin Rose playing the spy in the War—"

"Not *playing,*" the girl protested indignantly. "We both did useful work for the South."

That was a point which Winslow could not deny. Rose Greenhow and the girl facing him, Belle Boyd, had carried out their originally self-appointed—but soon officially recognized—duties in a most satisfactory manner. Each had achieved considerable fame and success. Gathering information had been Rose's forte. Belle had specialized in delivering the results of her cousin's work through the enemy's lines. Later, she had graduated to handling assignments of a tricky and frequently dangerous nature.* The Yankees had named her the Rebel Spy, and her efforts had caused them a great deal of trouble.

"I'm not gainsaying it," Winslow stated. "Vincent Boyd always wanted a son and at times I'll swear he had one."

"Why thank you 'most to death, as a good friend in Texas says," Belle replied, looking very feminine and not at all like anybody's *son*.

"Blast it, girl, he taught you to sit *astride* a horse and swore you could outride any man in Baton Royale County. He had you handling a sword and a gun when most girls of your age were playing with dolls—"

"Fencing and shooting were more fun," Belle interrupted. "And I always enjoyed savate lessons better than dancing. But mama saw to it that I didn't neglect the more ladylike accomplishments. If it hadn't been for Tollinger and Barmain, I'd probably have forgotten all about riding, shooting, and savate, married, and settled down to a life of dull respectability."

"Tollinger and Barmain!" Winslow snorted, knowing

* *Told in* The Colt and the Sabre, The Rebel Spy, *and* The Bloody Border.

them to have been the leaders of a drunken pro-Union rabble who had attacked the Boyd plantation before the start of the War. Belle's parents had been murdered and she was wounded. On her recovery, she had become a spy, seeking revenge against the pair. "If I could have laid my hands on them—"

"I did," Belle said quietly. "Down in Mexico, just after the War. In a way, that was how I joined the Secret Service."*

"I wondered why you insisted on going to the theater in disguise," Winslow commented, knowing that it was neither the time nor the place to seek further details of his niece's adventures.

"There wasn't time to explain. I only arrived this afternoon and knew that, as it was Sabot's last performance, whatever was due to happen must happen at it. I went in disguise because I wasn't sure if anybody would recognize me."

"You are after them?"

"Yes," Belle agreed, a touch defiantly. "Despite their loyalty to the South, I'm after them."

"*Loyalty!*" barked Winslow. "I yield second to no man in *my* loyalty to the South. But, by cracky, I fail to see how starting another war with the Yankees will help Dixie."

"Or me," Belle said quietly. "Uncle Alburgh, just how dangerous do you think the situation might be?"

"It could be very serious," Winslow replied. "Or it could fade into nothing. I'll have my paper treat it as no more than a stupid practical joke. After a night's cool and sober thought, I think that the rest of the audience will decide peace beats war any time. It'll all be forgotten in a week."

"Unless something happens to keep it in the public's eye," Belle warned.

"Such as?"

"I only wish I knew. They certainly didn't go to all that

* *Told in* Back to the Bloody Border.

trouble just to make a speech and then sit back and hope for developments. It's my belief that they plan to make sure their words aren't forgotten."

"How?" Winslow asked.

"I've no idea," the girl admitted. "But if the Frenchman is involved, it won't be pleasant—whatever it might be."

"The Frenchman?" Winslow repeated. "Is France the country to which the man kept referring?"

"I've no proof of that. I only know that this person called 'the Frenchman' is a leader in the plot. With the emphasis they placed on the Army's activities, it could be an incident involving the local soldiers. I hope that new commanding officer isn't delayed."

"He's here."

"And not too soon, from the stories I've heard. But that doesn't tell us why they held their meeting tonight."

"Perhaps they hoped to stir up trouble before Manderley took over?"

"It's possible," Belle conceded and stood up. "The answer might be at the theater. If so, I intend to find it."

Peeling off and dropping the mitts, Belle unfastened and removed her coat. She laid it on the seat and slipped out of the Balmoral skirt. That left her slender, willowy figure clad in an open-necked dark blue shirt, form-hugging black riding breeches, and calf-high Hessian boots. Nor did her unconventionally masculine attire end there. About her waist, previously concealed by the stiff, over-large skirt, was strapped a wide black leather gunbelt of Western fashion. Butt forward in the contoured holster, which was secured to her right thigh by pigging thongs, rode an ivory-handled Dance Bros. Navy revolver. Although percussion-primed and firing a .36-caliber combustible paper cartridge, it would still be an effective weapon in trained hands.

"I'll come with you," Winslow offered, studying her preparations.

"No, thank you," Belle refused.

"Blast it, girl. You can't go back there alone—"

"I can, and mean to. If I was looking for trouble, I'd welcome you. But I'm only going to scout around. And I can do that far safer alone."

"If all you're going to do is scout around," Winslow growled, "why don't you go back in your disguise?"

"If there's trouble, I don't want hindering by skirts," Belle explained. "And they wouldn't be any protection for me. The Frenchman wouldn't bother about me being a woman if he caught me."

"In that case, I'm coming with you!" Winslow stated.

"No, Uncle Alburgh!" Belle replied, speaking in a grim and definite manner. "I have to handle things my own way. This is my work. I wouldn't try to tell you how to run your newspaper or how to defend a law case. Anyway, there's probably nothing to find at the theater. But I'll feel easier if I've checked."

"Suppose there *is* something at the theater?" Winslow challenged.

"Then I'll do my level best to get away undetected," Belle promised with a smile. Becoming more serious, she continued, "You'll find an addressed envelope in my trunk. If I'm not back by morning, write a report of everything that has happened and mail it in the envelope."

"If you think that's all I'll do—"

"Very well. If I'm not back by midnight, go and tell the new commanding officer what's happened."

"Damn it! I'm going with you—" Winslow commenced. Then he shrugged. "Oh, do things your own way! You Boyd females have a most unseemly habit of doing as you please. I should know. I've married one. What if this Frenchman is there?"

"If he is and I get the chance," Belle answered, and her voice throbbed with cold, angry hatred, "I'll kill him."

Giving her uncle no opportunity to speak, Belle opened the door and dropped lightly to the sidewalk. She glanced in each direction, then strolled away. For all the emotion

he displayed, the aged Negro on the driving box might
have had an elderly woman enter and a slender, beautiful
girl emerge from his carriage every day of the week.

"Shall us wait for Miss Belle, Colonel?" Hector asked.

"No," Winslow replied, wondering why the note of
deadly hatred had come into his niece's voice each time
she had mentioned "the Frenchman." "Go home, Hector.
She'll come when she's finished her business."

Jerking back his head as the girl left the carriage, Hermy
felt certain that he had escaped being observed by her. He
peeped cautiously around the corner and saw her turning
to walk off in the opposite direction. Frowning, he swung
on his heel to return to the waiting buggy.

"I don't know where the hell she come from," Hermy
told Matt in wondering tones, "but a gal wearing pants just
got out of Winslow's carriage."

"A gal, *wearing pants!*" the burly man repeated, eyeing
his companion with cold suspicion. "What're you try—"

"Go see for yourself," Hermy suggested.

"Which way did she go?" Matt demanded, making as if
to leave his seat and follow the other's suggestion.

"Back the way she come. Here's Winslow's carriage."

"We'll keep going after him," Matt decided, sinking
back on to the seat.

"How about the gal?" Hermy inquired, unaware of certain suspicions he was arousing. "She might be headed
back to the theater."

"All right," Matt grunted. "You go watch her. I'll tend to
Winslow."

"What do I do if she is headed for the theater?" Hermy
wanted to know.

"Make sure she doesn't come away alive," Matt replied
and set the buggy into motion.

# 4

# A NATIONAL DISASTER

*Belle Boyd's deep and bitter hatred for the person she knew only as "the Frenchman" had had its beginning aboard the Mississippi riverboat* Elegant Lady, *as it lay alongside a dock at Memphis before continuing south to New Orleans.*

"There's a gennelman to see you, Miss Winslow," announced the colored stewardess, entering Belle's stateroom on the *Elegant Lady* and using the name under which the girl was traveling.

Telling the Negro woman to show the gentleman in, Belle wondered who he might be and, more important, what he wanted with her. That he was in the Secret Service seemed obvious from his knowing her assumed name.

Taking a well-earned vacation, after completing an assignment that had not been without danger, she was on her way to New Orleans. Of course, her superiors had been informed of her destination and the route by which she would be traveling. Every Secret Service organization insisted upon keeping in touch with its members, even when they were taking a holiday. Given luck, the visitor would only be another agent paying a friendly courtesy call.

That hope ended abruptly with her first sight of the visitor.

Soberly and plainly dressed, the man was below middle

height, lean, and with a prissy, self-important air. He looked like the owner, or manager, of a successful business —arrogant, within the bounds of his power, to underlings and a stickler for protocol as it affected himself. Belle recognized him as Alden H. Stenhouse, senior coordinator of the Secret Service along the middle reaches of the Mississippi River.

One thing was for sure. Stenhouse was not the kind of man who would pay a purely social call to a mere agent— even to one of Belle's prominence.

"Good afternoon, Miss B—Miss Winslow," Stenhouse greeted, looking uneasy.

"Good afternoon, Mr. Stenhouse," the girl answered, knowing that he would not be traveling under an assumed name. "Can I have the stewardess bring you a drink or anything?"

"No, thank you," Stenhouse refused. "I have come to see you on a confidential matter of some importance."

"Feel free to do it," Belle drawled as the stewardess left the stateroom and closed the door. "The boat doesn't sail for three hours."

"You won't be leaving with it," Stenhouse warned brusquely, as if wanting to get things straight immediately.

"I won't?" asked Belle, a hint of challenge in her voice.

"No," Stenhouse stated. Another, bigger man might have tempered the word with a more polite, apologetic refusal. Conscious of his authority, he made no attempt to do so. "I have an assignment for you."

"You realize, of course, that I'm on vacation?" Belle demanded, annoyed by his behavior.

"General Handiman assured me that you would be willing to return to duty," the man replied, wanting to impress upon her that his demand carried top-grade, official backing. "This is a matter of considerable importance, Miss Boyd. I can't overestimate just *how* vital it is. In fact, it might even develop into a national disaster."

"Sit down and tell me about it," Belle suggested, curiosity overriding any resentment she felt at the intrusion, or over Stenhouse's attitude.

"I hardly know where to begin," the man admitted, taking a seat.

"They do say that the beginning's the best place to start," Belle commented. "And the more I know, the better I can handle my part in it."

"I suppose the beginning was in Topeka, Kansas," Stenhouse said, producing a notebook from his jacket's inside pocket and flipping it open. "But we aren't concerned with that—"

"Not even if it helps me see the full picture?" Belle interrupted, more to annoy her visitor than for any special reason. "I'd hate to keep asking for you to clear up some point I haven't heard about."

"Very well," Stenhouse sniffed. "A group of Topeka businessmen, in early 'Sixty-Five, decided that they would raise a regiment of cavalry—"

"They left it late in the day," Belle commented, for that had been the year which had seen the end of military hostilities.

"Probably they hadn't foreseen how close we were to victory," Stenhouse replied tactlessly. Realizing that the girl might not be pleased with the reference to the South's defeat, he nevertheless did not offer to apologize. "Anyway, they set about organizing what would have been the 18th 'Kansas' Dragoons."

*"Dragoons?"*

"It would have been in name only. They were to be equipped with Burnside hats and standard uniforms and accoutrements, but armed with Henry rifles."

"That would have cost money," Belle remarked.

"Yes," conceded Stenhouse. "Most of it would have been raised by public subscriptions. However, what with one delay or another, the War ended before the Dragoons had acquired their full requirements. In fact, they had obtained only sufficient uniforms and arms for one hundred men. Although the businessmen canceled the rest of their orders, they had to purchase those which had been filled. So they found themselves stuck with the rifles and equipment."

"I feel for them," Belle said dryly. "Why didn't they sell them?"

"There was no market for surplus military equipment when they decided to do so. It's my belief that they hung on hoping to have their regiment retained on a permanent basis, but failed to do so. They left it too late to dispose of even the Henry rifles at so much as their cost price."

"The new, improved Winchester Model of 1866 certainly reduced the value of the Henry," Belle admitted. "So what did the speculators do?"

"They held on, hoping for the opportunity to dispose of their purchases at, if not a profit, something close to the original cost."

"Which they eventually managed?"

"Yes. Two men, calling themselves Duprez and le Beausainte, made an acceptable offer. They said that they were commissioned by the legislature of Oregon to purchase arms and equipment for the State's militia. Their price was satisfactory and the spec—businessmen didn't check on the story. However, one of their number had misgivings. What nationality do the names Duprez and le Beausainte suggest to you, Miss Boyd?"

"French or Creole," the girl replied without hesitation. "But the speculator had reasons to doubt that they were either."

"Yes," Stenhouse confirmed. "Their accents were unmistakably—*Irish!*"

"Huh huh!" Belle said noncommittally, although she could guess in which direction the conversation was heading.

"Fortunately the spec—businessman had the good sense to mention his misgivings to a U.S. marshal who was in Topeka at the time," Stenhouse went on, studiously avoiding the term "speculator" when mentioning the Kansas citizens. "Marshal Cole—"

"Solly Cole?" Belle interrupted.

"Yes. Of course, you worked with him."

"I did. He's a smart lawman."*

"Smart enough to see the implications in the disparity between the two men's names and their accents," Stenhouse agreed. "You understand my meaning?"

"Yes," Belle replied. "I understand."

In 1872, the international membership of the *Alabama* Arbitration Tribunal had completed its long investigations and deliberations. It had rendered a decision most favorable to the United States. For permitting the Confederate States' naval cruisers like the *Alabama, Florida,* and *Shenandoah* to be built in and operate from their ports—as well as being involved in other activities which had aided the South—the Government of Great Britain had been ordered to pay compensation to the tune of $77,500,000.

Since that event, the U.S. Congress had trodden very warily where British interests were concerned. Given an opportunity, the British would be only too willing to invoke a similar international body and try to retrieve some of the money. In general, Congress realized that Ireland and British-Irish affairs might easily supply the required excuse.

Over the years, large numbers of Irish nationals had emigrated to the United States. While a few might have fled to escape persecution or to avoid the consequences for acts of political violence, the majority had merely come in search of new homes and a higher standard of living. The love which many of them expressed for the "ould country" had increased enormously with the distance they had put between themselves and it.

Although many of the emigrants had frequently discussed "liberating" Ireland from British domination, only

* *Details of Marshal Solly Cole's career are given in* Calamity Spells Trouble.

some of the wealthier and better educated—who may have been motivated by thoughts of great opportunities for social, business, or political advancement as "saviors" of their native land—had turned their attention to actively achieving that end.

So far, however, the efforts of the Irish-American "loyalists" had not reached noticeable proportions. Politicians of Irish descent had frequently attempted to invoke official action by the United States against British rule. For one reason or another, every session of Congress had refused to sanction such measures.

With the commencement of the *Alabama* Arbitration Tribunal, there had been a growing awareness of the danger to chances of a satisfactory decision if even unofficial intervention in Irish affairs should be launched from the United States. So General Philo Handiman, head of the Secret Service, had been ordered to stay alert for, and to prevent, such incidents.

"Marshal Cole telegraphed the story to General Handiman," Stenhouse went on. "He also instituted inquiries in Salem. The Oregon legislature had not commissioned the two men. Nor, Cole learned, had the consignment been sent west. It was taken to Kansas City and sent down the Missouri to St. Louis. One of our agents was waiting for its arrival and traveled on the same boat to Memphis. Once here, the consignment was disembarked and placed into a warehouse owned by Phineas Molloy, who is Irish."

"He certainly doesn't sound French," Belle could not resist remarking.

"My agent—" Stenhouse continued stiffly.

"Does he have a name?" Belle interrupted.

"It's Horatio A. Darren. Do you know him?"

"We haven't met," Belle replied, tactfully refraining from mentioning that she had heard of Horatio A. Darren and was aware of his relationship to Stenhouse. "What has he been doing?"

"He kept watch on the warehouse for two days, but the boxes carrying the consignment weren't brought out again. So, last night after it was closed, he broke in and examined them."

"What did he learn?"

"That they are still sealed and are marked 'To Await Collection.' "

"Nothing else?"

"What else could he learn?" Stenhouse demanded. "He didn't want them to know he'd been there, and he could hardly have made a more detailed examination without leaving traces of his presence."

"I should have seen that," Belle drawled. "But where do I come in?"

"Hora—Agent Darren may need assistance," Stenhouse explained, looking evasive but sounding as if he doubted that such a need could ever arise. "So General Handiman suggested, as you were in the vicinity, that I should make use of your services."

"Why, I just hope that I can live up to your trust, sir," Belle said, with such humble sincerity that she might have been speaking the truth.

"Shall we go and make a start?" Stenhouse asked.

"There's one problem," Belle objected. "When I came aboard, my trunk was placed in the hold. I wasn't expecting to need it, and getting it out again before New Orleans will be inconvenient for the captain."

"Is it imperative that you have it?"

"Most of my equipment is in it—wigs, special clothing, things I need for disguises—"

"You won't need any of them," Stenhouse assured her. "All I need is for you to assist Hor—Agent Darren. In all probability you'll be able to continue your journey on the next boat. We, of course, will defray any expenses this puts you to—within reason."

"Why thank you 'most to death," Belle said sardonically.

"You can start by paying for a telegraph message I'm going to send."

"To whom?"

"A friend in New Orleans. She can collect and hold my trunk when the *Elegant Lady* arrives. I'll arrange with the captain for it to be handed over."

"Is your friend trustworthy?" Stenhouse wanted to know.

"If she isn't, somebody's made a bad mistake," Belle replied. "It's Madame Lucienne and she's with the Secret Service, just like us. Where do I meet Hora—Agent Darren, Mr. Stenhouse?"

# 5
# I'LL PROTECT YOU,
# MISS BOYD

Belle Boyd had not been impressed by Stenhouse and she found herself even less inspired by his nephew. Neatly dressed in a gray suit of the latest Eastern fashion, white shirt with one of the newfangled celluloid collars and a sober blue tie, Horatio A. Darren was tall, brown-haired, reasonably handsome—although dark lines under his eyes suggested that he had been losing sleep recently—and had an athletic build. A revolver raised a noticeable lump under the left side of his vest—being the more noticeable due to his habit of drawing attention to the protuberance by a variety of gestures. There was about him an air of smug, self-satisfied, complacent superiority that the girl found both amusing and irritating. Going by his response when his uncle had performed the introductions, Darren clearly considered that the affair was firmly under his control, and it was obvious that he resented Belle's intrusion.

For all that, Darren had struggled to prevent his feelings from showing. He was torn between the desire to impress his attractive visitor and his annoyance that anybody could believe *he* would require assistance on any assignment. Helped along by Belle's appearance and attitude, the former emotion won.

All in all, Belle presented an attractive picture. She wore

the normal traveling garb of a well-to-do, fashionable lady. The brown two-piece jacket and Balmoral skirt set off her slender, shapely figure, just as the small, neat hat and brown wig—the latter to prevent her short black hair from drawing attention—combined to accentuate the beautiful lines of her face. However, the garments concealed a dark blue shirt, black riding breeches, and Hessian boots. These had all been available in her stateroom aboard the *Elegant Lady*. Having been made to her measure by a master cobbler, the boots were so comfortable that she preferred them to more conventional footwear and had had them on her feet when Stenhouse had arrived. Her gunbelt and the Dance Bros. Navy revolver had been in her trunk aboard the riverboat. So, if she should need a weapon, she would have to rely upon the Remington Double Derringer in her vanity bag or the specially designed parasol which dangled negligently in her right hand.

The meeting was taking place in a room hired by Darren, at a small hotel which stood across the street from Molloy's warehouse.

After Belle had packed such of her belongings as were in the stateroom and made arrangements for the disposal of the rest of her property, she had accompanied Stenhouse to the Travelers Hotel. An expensive, new establishment, the hotel had two advantages. One, it was close to the river and much used by travelers with money to meet its high tariff; two, neither Stenhouse nor his nephew resided there. Having settled in and, while an impatient Stenhouse waited in the foyer, changed into her male attire, Belle had been escorted by him to the rendezvous. With the introductions performed, Stenhouse had left the agents to their own devices.

"Come to the window, Miss Boyd," Darren requested briskly, as the door closed on his departing uncle. The words came out as an order, for he wanted to establish who was running things. "You can see the consignment from it.

I don't need to tell *you* to make sure that you're not seen looking, do I?"

"Why I'm *so* pleased to have you remind me of that," the girl purred, dripping honey spiked with strychnine in every word. "I might have spoiled all your good work if you hadn't."

Eyeing Belle speculatively, Darren could read only what he took for an expression of respectful admiration. Being a young man with more than his fair share of ego, he preferred to accept that it *was* her true feeling about him. He felt certain that he was making a satisfactory impression on her, both as an expert in their mutual trade and as a masterful member of the stronger, dominant sex.

Ignoring Darren, except to follow his unnecessary advice regarding concealment, Belle stood alongside the window and looked cautiously across the street. The double main doors of the warehouse were wide open. Through them, to the rear but in plain sight, she could see four oblong and two square wooden boxes of the kind used for transporting quantities of rifles and ammunition. Near by were four large bales less easy to identify.

"There they are!" Darren announced dramatically, exposing himself far more than Belle did. "Four boxes, twenty-five rifles to the box. Five thousand .44 rimfire bullets in each of the square boxes. The hats, uniforms, boots, and accoutrements are in the bales."

"Huh huh!" Belle said, still studying the interior of the warehouse. "They've been there like that ever since they came from the boat?"

"Yes. I've had them under observation all the time."

"Do they leave the doors open at night?"

"Of course not!" Darren snapped, scanning the beautiful features for traces of the faintly sarcastic undertones he had thought he detected in her voice. "But I keep watch at night and make patrols around the warehouse at intervals."

"Mercy!" Belle gasped, understanding the cause of the dark lines under his eyes. "When do you sleep?"

"During the day. But I've got one of Molloy's men working for me. He's to let me know as soon as anybody comes to collect the consignment."

"I see," Belle drawled. Although she would have liked to go further into how Darren had made such a fortunate acquaintance, she decided against it. Her instincts warned that to do so would antagonize him and ruin all hope of willing cooperation. "So all we need to do is wait for whoever comes to make the collection."

"That's all," Darren agreed. "There wasn't any real need for Unc—them to delay your vacation, Miss Boyd. Not that I don't appreciate your coming to he—to work with me."

"Why thank you, 'most to death," Belle purred. "I hope that I can be useful. Is there any way I could take a closer look at the consignment?"

*"I've* already done *that!"* Darren pointed out.

"Couldn't I take just a little peek, so I can feel I'm doing something worthwhile?"

"You couldn't enter as I did. I used a ladder to reach the hayloft's loading door, slipped its fastener, and got in through it."

"Couldn't I do that?" Belle wanted to know. "With *your* help of course?"

When Belle Boyd put on her most appealing manner, she could charm even a less egoistical and susceptible man than Darren. Wanting to impress her, he felt that a visit to the warehouse would be a big step in the required direction.

"I suppose you could, if you can climb the ladder," he conceded.

"I think I could do that," Belle replied, sounding uncertain. "Isn't there a watchman?"

"No. Don't worry. If there's any trouble, I'll protect you, Miss Boyd."

At that moment, several men emerged from the warehouse. They swung the big doors shut and one of their number turned. Waving a hand, he crossed the street in the direction of the hotel. Tall, lean, with a tanned, heavily moustached face, he wore similar style clothing to the men he had left—that of a poorly paid worker.

"That's O'Reilly," Darren commented, indicating the man. "Now they've closed for the day, he's coming to report."

"He comes straight over here—" Belle began.

"By the rear entrance," Darren elaborated. "It would arouse suspicions if he used the front door."

"I can see that it might," Belle conceded. "Perhaps it would be better if he didn't see me."

"He's quite trustworthy—"

"I don't doubt it. But I don't need to tell *you* how much of an advantage it will be if nobody other than ourselves learns I'm involved."

"That's true," Darren agreed. "Perhaps you can hide in the wardrobe?"

"It won't be necessary," Belle replied. "I'll leave now, before he arrives, and go back to my hotel. I'll come later this evening and see the warehouse."

"That would be best," Darren confirmed, crossing to open the door.

Leaving the room, Belle hurried along the passage. She heard footsteps in the hall below, so went by the head of the stairs to halt at a door. Facing it, she bent her legs, bowed her shoulders and made as if she was searching for the key in her vanity bag. O'Reilly reached the top of the stairs, darted a glance in her direction, and went to Darren's door. Letting the man disappear inside, Belle straightened up and descended to the ground floor. Leaving the hotel, she crossed the street and halted so that she could see inside to the foot of the stairs.

Apparently O'Reilly had not brought an extensive report that afternoon. He soon came into view on the stairs. Despite his earlier precaution of making the visit via the rear door, he left through the front entrance. Belle followed him as he strode off along the street.

As she walked, Belle wondered if she might be wasting her time. Perhaps she was allowing first impressions to influence her against Darren. He could have been lucky—or shrewd—enough to find a corruptible member of Molloy's warehouse staff. Yet, for all that, Belle could not throw off her feeling that all was far from being well. Everything seemed to be happening just too conveniently—the boxes being placed in plain view and Darren finding the right man to keep him informed. Belle was suspicious by nature and training. Of an active temperament, she always believed in taking the most direct means of satisfying her curiosity.

Belle had not been following the man for long before she decided that her misgivings might have some foundation. Instead of making for the section of town in which one of his class might be expected to live, O'Reilly directed his steps toward the higher-rent district. Much to her surprise, Belle watched him pass through the portals of the Travelers Hotel. That was hardly the kind of establishment in which a poorly paid warehouse attendant would live. Yet he was clearly known there. The desk clerk handed over a room key without question or comment. Allowing O'Reilly to disappear up the stairs, Belle entered and went to the desk.

"Was that workman going near my room?" she inquired. "If so, I hope he isn't going to make a lot of noise."

"Workman?" the clerk queried, then smiled. "You must mean Mr. Sheriff." He dropped his voice to a confidential whisper. "It's all right, Miss Winslow, he's not a workman. He's a Pinkerton detective in disguise."

*"Mercy!"* Belle gasped, sounding suitably impressed. "Who-all's he after, somebody at the hotel?"

"Certainly not!" gasped the clerk. "He's heard that the James gang is planning a robbery and is keeping watch for them down by the river."

"I just hope he catches them," Belle said and, wanting to avoid having her interest in "Sheriff" mentioned, went on, "and I surely hope you don't tell him about my foolish mistake. Why, I'd be right mortified if you did."

"I won't say a word, Miss Winslow," the clerk promised.

Probably, Belle told herself as she crossed to the dining room, because he had realized that he might be regarded as having been indiscreet in discussing "Sheriff's" occupation with another guest.

Selecting a table which would allow her to see O'Reilly —or Sheriff—if he returned downstairs, Belle ordered a meal. She pondered upon the remarkable coincidence— which no author would dare to let happen in his stories— of O'Reilly using her hotel. Then she decided that the man had probably selected it, as she had, for its high standard of comfort and proximity to the docks. One thing was for sure. O'Reilly was no ordinary, if disloyal, warehouse employee. Belle could imagine that Darren's surveillance had aroused somebody's suspicions. So O'Reilly had made his acquaintance and was ensuring that he saw only what the conspirators wanted him to see.

The question, to Belle's way of thinking, was, why should they go to all that trouble?

Learning the reason struck the girl as being one of the things which must be done. Perhaps the visit to the warehouse would provide her with the answer.

O'Reilly had not made an appearance by the time Belle had finished her meal. Noticing that the clerk was not behind the desk, she crossed to it and turned the register around. A quick examination told her the number of O'Reilly's room and that he had come to the hotel on the same day that the consignment arrived in Memphis. Replacing the book, Belle went up to the first floor. In passing, she paused to listen at O'Reilly's door and heard him moving about. Then she went to her own quarters.

Deciding that they must deal with O'Reilly the following day, Belle gave thought to her examination of the consignment. She had no intention, except as a last resort, of entering the warehouse by the route which Darren had suggested. However, she meant to conduct the investigation wearing suitable clothing.

Removing her hat and wig, Belle took them to the wardrobe. She placed them inside and brought out the long black cloak which hung there. With that on and the hood raised, she could dispense with the coat and skirt as covering for her male garments.

Having removed her feminine attire and placed it, with the vanity bag and parasol, in the wardrobe, she thrust the Remington Double Derringer into her waistband. Then she donned the cloak and raised its hood. A look in the wardrobe's mirror satisfied her that she could get by in her unconventional attire, especially as night had fallen, and not arouse unwanted interest in her appearance.

Dressed and equipped for the work which lay ahead, Belle prepared to go and do it. Glancing along the passage as she emerged, she saw that the door of O'Reilly's room was opening. A subconscious reflex action caused Belle to retreat into her room and almost close the door. Peering through the crack she had left, she was grateful that she had taken such a precaution. On coming out, O'Reilly proved to have changed his clothes. Now he was dressed more in keeping with a resident at an expensive hotel. Settling a bowler hat on his head, he made for the stairs. His appearance and attitude implied that he was leaving the building rather than merely going down to the dining room.

"Fortune favors the fair," Belle mused, allowing O'Reilly to pass out of sight before stepping into the passage. "Twice in one day. It can't last."

Belle waited until the man had reached the ground floor before starting down the stairs. Already she had decided to revise her plans. There would be ample time later to follow the original arrangements. In fact, the visit to the warehouse could not be undertaken until after midnight. So she considered that she would be more usefully employed in trying to learn more about O'Reilly.

By the time Belle reached the foyer, her quarry had gone out of the front door. She followed as he strolled along the sidewalk. Using all her skill, she stayed close enough to make sure that she did not lose sight of O'Reilly, yet at a sufficient distance to prevent him detecting her presence. The night was warm and starlit, but not many people were on the streets. For all that, Belle felt certain the man had not located her. She hoped that he would remain on foot. If he should take a carriage, she might have difficulty in obtaining one in which to continue her surveillance.

Fortune still appeared to be favoring the fair. O'Reilly kept walking, passing into the business and entertainment section of the poorer part of the city. Then he turned down an alley by the Bijou Theater. If the darkened, deserted aspect of the building was anything to go on, there was no show that night. Belle arrived at the mouth of the alley in time to see him turn at the rear of the theater. Stepping quietly, she reached and peered around the corner. Unlocking what would probably be the stage door, O'Reilly paused. He struck a match, found and lit a lamp which had been hanging near the door. Going in, he drew the door closed behind him.

Moving even more cautiously, Belle advanced to the door. A faint glow of light showed as she bent to the keyhole. Squinting through it, she watched the man enter one of the row of dressing rooms. There was no other sign of life in the darkened building. So Belle decided that she would try to take O'Reilly prisoner. If she did, she felt sure that she could induce him to answer questions.

Twisting at the door's handle, she pushed gently. Nothing happened. A cluck of annoyance broke from the girl. Either the lock was one of the newfangled variety that operated automatically, or O'Reilly had turned and taken away the key on entering.

At least, Belle hoped that it was only the lock which held the door against her push. If O'Reilly had shot the bolts on the inside, she would not be able to effect an entrance at that point.

On the other hand, providing that the lock was of the comparatively uncomplicated standard variety—as seemed most likely in such an old building—Belle felt certain that she could accomplish something. One of the subjects in which she had taken training, in the Secret Service of both the South and the United States, had been how to open locks for which she did not possess the formal key.

Shoving firmly at first the top then the bottom of the door, Belle felt it yield a little on each occasion. That implied it was secured in the center, at the region of the lock. Wishing that she dare strike a match and make a closer examination, she ran the tip of her right forefinger over the surface of the keyhole.

"It's a lever, I'd say," she mused. "Let's hope that I stay lucky and it's been cut for a master key."

While Belle had proved a ready learner, when being instructed by an expert in the art of picking open locks, she was aware of her limitations in that line. Given time, she could probably manipulate the mechanism of an ordinary lever lock. If it should have been equipped with the accessory she mentioned, her chances of success would be considerably improved.

A "lever" lock was operated by a series of small plates which fitted into the grooves of the bolt and prevented it from sliding. Each of the plates, or levers, had a notch in its end that corresponded with the notches of the key. When the key was turned, the pressure would raise all the levers to their correct positions and permit the bolt to function.

What Belle hoped to find was the addition of a master key's lever. Set beyond the reach of the ordinary key, the "master" lever was adjusted to operate all the other plates. It was a device often used in public buildings, allowing the janitor, or other persons in possession of a master key, to enter several rooms without the necessity of carrying a bunch of individual keys.

Reaching into the V-shaped notch at the front of her left boot with her thumb and the tip of her forefinger, Belle drew a useful little tool from its sheath. It was a piece of thick, stiff wire about four inches in length and shaped like a miniature hockey stick.

Guiding the implement into the keyhole, Belle tested the interior of the lock. Under her gentle pressure, she felt something give a little. Twisting at the pick, she caused the master lever to perform its function. There was a faint click and the door moved in response to her push. Before opening it fully, she returned the pick to the sheath in the Hessian boot. That left her hands unencumbered and ready for use in her defense if the need arose. However, she wanted to have complete freedom of movement. So she reached up to unfasten her cloak.

Then a thought struck Belle.

If O'Reilly had locked the door behind him, why had he taken out the key?

Most likely because somebody else was coming and would wish to gain admittance.

The realization came just too late.

Belle heard a faint sound close behind her. Then a hand caught hold of her left shoulder and swung her around. Something hard crashed into the side of her jaw before she could think of protecting herself. For a moment bright lights seemed to be bursting inside her skull. Then everything went dark and she crumpled limply to the ground.

# 6
# YOU'RE GOING TO TELL US
# *EVERYTHING*

"Who the hell is she and where did she come from?" demanded a man's voice, hard, rasping, yet educated Southern in its timbre.

"Don't ask me," replied a second set of male tones, higher pitched and less definable by accent. "It's strange, but I've had a feeling all day that somebody was watching me."

"I know it's not likely, but she could have come here looking for *you*," suggested the first speaker. "It's pretty well known that you're playing here tonight."

"She was following *you*, I tell you," protested the other man, sounding almost femininely petulant. "I saw you coming along the street and was just going to call out when I spotted her. There was something in the way she acted that made me keep quiet. Sure enough, she followed you down the alley. And she was just coming in here when I sneaked up and dealt with her."

"I locked the blasted door behind me!"

"She had got it opened—some way."

Wishing they would stop, as the words seemed to be pounding like hammer blows inside her head, Belle Boyd lay listening to the conversation. At first, the voices had seemed to be coming from a long way off; but they were rapidly drawing closer. Everything about her appeared to be sheltering in a swirling cloud of mist. Then a faint light pricked its way through, growing brighter until it started to hurt her eyes. Groaning a little, she tried to shield them from the glare. When she began to raise her right hand, the left stubbornly insisted on going with it for some reason.

Dull pain, throbbing in the region of her jaw, brought Belle to a partial realization of her predicament. Then a fuller sense of understanding assailed her. Thoughts flooded through her disturbed senses, warning her that her situation might be desperate.

Belle became aware that she was lying on her back upon a hard, bare wooden floor. Raising her head slightly, she discovered why her hands had functioned in unison. While she had been unconscious, her captors had crossed her right wrist over the left and lashed them firmly together with a gaily colored silk scarf. There was one bright aspect; her arms were bound at the front and not behind her back. An experiment told her that her legs were still free.

The mists cleared completely and Belle gazed about her. What she saw, by the light of a lamp which stood on a table in what must be a dressing room of the Bijou Theater, was not calculated to lessen her forebodings and perturbation. The speakers were standing, gazing down at her. One she identified as O'Reilly—or "Sheriff"—and he was scowling in a puzzled, menacing manner.

Not quite as tall as his companion, the second man was slender, with a pallid, weakly handsome face. He was dressed tidily, even fussily, in a black frock coat, frilly-bosomed and -cuffed white silk shirt, multi-colored cravat, tight white trousers, and highly polished town boots. His right hand toyed with a Remington Double Derringer which Belle recognized as being from her waistband.

From studying her captors, Belle completed her examination of the room. It was meagerly furnished with the dressing table and two chairs. In the left rear corner, her

cloak was hanging over a large trunk which bore the inscription, "DEXTER OPAL. Eccentric Tramp, Juggler,
and Distinguished Comedian."

"Ah!" said the slender man, his voice high with excitement. "Our mysterious visitor has awakened."

"I bet you was worrying in case *you* had to be Prince
Charming and kiss her," O'Reilly answered dryly, then addressed Belle. "Why did you follow me here?"

"I—I don't know what you mean," Belle replied, wrig-
gling into a sitting position with her back resting against
the wall at the hinged side of the door. "Wh-why have you
brought me here?"

"She doesn't know, Opal," O'Reilly mocked.

"It won't work, girlie," Dexter Opal warned. "*You* know
why we brought you here. Now *we* want to know why *you*
came. You're going to tell us *everything* we want to know.
And it will be a whole lot less painful, if not as much fun
for us, if you do it right away."

"I—I don't kn-know wh-what you mean," Belle bluffed
—and was called.

"And I hate to be lied to, girlie!" Opal hissed, advancing
to drive his right foot viciously in the direction of Belle's
body.

Having seen the play of emotion on the juggler's face,
the girl had read his intentions. So she responded swiftly
and with perfect timing. Flinging herself sideways, she
avoided the kick. Grazing her shoulder in passing, Opal's
toes impacted against the wall. A tinny screech of pain
burst from him. Hopping on his left leg, he grabbed at the
right's boot. Then fury distorted his features. Slamming his
foot to the floor, he thrust forward the Remington.

"Quit that, damn you!" O'Reilly ordered, catching his
companion by the shoulder roughly and jerking him away
from the girl. "She's got to answer some questions for us."

"I'll make her answer, damn you!" Opal promised almost hysterically, twisting his shoulder from the other's
grasp. "I'll make her beg to answer."

"Not here, blast it!" O'Reilly fumed, holding his arm across the other's chest and restraining him. "She could have people looking out for her. Besides which, *they'll* soon be arriving for the meeting."

"We could have the answers before they get here," Opal protested, glaring malevolently in Belle's direction.

"I wouldn't want to bet on it," O'Reilly answered, watching Belle return to a sitting position. "She's not as scared as she wants us to believe. I'll bet she'd be a hard nut to crack."

"Just leave me at her," Opal suggested eagerly. "I'll soon enough crack her for you."

"I'll just bet you would, Tiger," O'Reilly grinned. "But not here. We'll take her to a cabin I know in the woods, and you can go do it after the meeting."

"You mean you're going to leave her here until then?"

"No. We'll take her there now. It'll be safer that way."

"How do we do it, *walk?*"

"There's a livery barn along the street," O'Reilly replied. "Go fetch a rig and we'll take her in that."

"You go and fetch it," Opal snarled, showing his resentment at the other man's disparaging attitude.

"Why me?" O'Reilly challenged.

"Because I've a better reason than you have for being in here, if anybody belonging to this rat trap comes."

"There's that to it. Will you be all right until I get back?"

"If you mean, can I handle her?" Opal purred, studying Belle with cold, cruel eyes, "just let her try anything on with me and *she'll* soon enough learn the answer."

"I'll fasten her ankles and gag her be—" O'Reilly offered.

Tensing, Belle prepared to make a desperate fight rather than submit to having her legs secured. During the conversation, she had studied her bonds and believed that—given a suitable opportunity—she could unfasten the knot with her teeth. However, she knew that the men might do a

better job and, with her legs bound, she would have no
hope of escape.

"I can do that," Opal assured his companion, solving the
problem for Belle. "You fetch the buggy. We don't have
that much time to spare. And if she has friends who'll be
looking for her, the sooner she's away from here the better."

"You're right," O'Reilly admitted, reluctantly. "I'll get
back as quickly as I can."

"You don't sound Irish," Belle commented, as they
heard the man close and lock the stage door. She wanted
to delay the gagging as long as possible, in the hope that
she might raise the alarm. "If it comes to that, neither does
O'Reilly."

"Hah!" Opal said, slapping his thigh triumphantly as if
he had made an important discovery. "*You're* working with
that fool who's watching the warehouse."

"*Do* you know who *he's* working for?" Belle challenged.

If her estimation of Darren's character was correct, the
girl felt sure that he could not have resisted trying to impress O'Reilly by disclosing his official status.

"The Secret Service, he says," Opal replied, confirming
Belle's supposition. "They must be short of men." He
paused and eyed her in a speculative manner. "You're a
Southron, aren't you?"

"Yes. But I'm also in the Secret Service. Your principals
won't like it if you kill me—"

"Don't count on it," the juggler jeered. "They'd probably call you a traitress."

"Why?" Belle inquired, genuinely puzzled by the comment.

"That's for me to know and you to find out," Opal replied, with the air of one who had realized that he was on
the verge of being indiscreet. "Not that you'll get the
chance to find anything out."

Watching the slender man, Belle decided against taking
any action at that moment. She wanted to be sure that

O'Reilly was out of hearing range before she made her bid to escape. Until then, she meant to do all she could to lull Opal into a sense of false security. She guessed that she could keep him talking and divert his thoughts from completing the binding and gagging.

"Why are *you* involved in this business?" Belle inquired. "You're not Irish, so it can't be for national reasons. Are you a Catholic?"

"Like hell I am!"

"Then that rules out religious motives. So it's for money—"

"Put your ankles together—"

"If it's for money," Belle said, obeying, "I can get you as much—in fact, even *more*—than they're paying you."

"*You* can?" Opal asked, halting as he started to back away.

"Certainly," Belle confirmed. "All you have to do is set me free—"

"And trust you to fill my hands with gold?" Opal sneered.

"Why not?" Belle countered. "I don't want to die. And besides—"

"Yes?" Opal prompted, making no attempt to start tying her up.

"We're determined to break up this crowd you're working for. So we'd pay well for any information you could give us. And even better if you could help to place one of our people in their organization."

Clearly Opal was interested in the idea. Belle watched his brows crease and knew that he was turning it over in his mind. Frowning, he closed the dressing room's door. Much to her delight, he still made no attempt to carry out further bondage.

"Stay where you are!" Opal warned, jerking up the Remington as the girl made as if to rise. "I don't trust you."

"But you like my proposition," Belle guessed.

"It's a stupid idea," Opal complained. "How do I explain when Ga—O'Reilly tells them I've let you escape?"

"We'll make sure that he *can't* tell them."

"You mean *kill* him?"

"That won't trouble you, the way he treats you," Belle drawled.

"You're right!" Opal spat, mentally recalling all the insults and humiliation he had suffered at O'Reilly's hands.

"I know how you feel," Belle said sympathetically. "I like *girls* and I've had some of it."

"I knew you *were!*" Opal breathed, eyes raking her from head to toe. "Your hair, those clothes . . . Can I trust you? Will your people do as you say?"

"Of course. With fifteen and a half million dollars at stake, they can afford to be generous."

"Fifteen and a half million . . . ?"

"I see *they* don't trust you enough to tell you *everything,*" Belle smiled. "They're willing to *use* you, but they despise you because . . . Well, that's what they could cost the United States if their plot succeeds. So we can afford to pay you handsomely."

"Shut up!" Opal hissed, showing that her reference to the money had both puzzled and interested him. "I want to think this thing out."

"Go ahead, but think carefully," Belle advised. "We're on to that crowd's game. And we're not all as stupid as Mr. Darren *pretends* to be. It's only a matter of time before we lay our hands on *everybody* concerned in it."

"I said shut up!" Opal snarled, menacing her with the Remington pistol. "Stay right where you are."

"Time's running out, but I can wait," Belle drawled, settling down as if she felt sure that the result was a foregone conclusion. "Just so long as you've decided *before* O'Reilly comes back."

Stepping to the rear without taking his eyes from Belle, still gripping the Remington in a threatening manner, Opal hooked his rump daintily onto the edge of the table. Belle could sense the wavering of his attitude. If she guessed correctly, he was debating which line of action would be most advantageous to him.

Should he remain loyal to his employers, or would he be safer and better off if he accepted Belle's offer?

Belle knew that her fate, in fact her very life, hung on the answer.

Almost two minutes dragged by in silence, with Belle allowing Opal to stew in his own juices and draw his own conclusions. She had done all she could to lead him in the right direction. Playing upon his obvious greed, she had also reminded him of the contempt with which O'Reilly—and probably others—had regarded his homosexual tendencies. She had also established a bond with him by pretending to be a lesbian and, as such, understanding his problems.

Now everything rested in Opal's hands. Belle sensed that any further prompting from a woman, even one he assumed to be a lesbian, might turn him from the proposal. On the other hand, her hint that Darren might not be the dupe Opal imagined and the comment on the Secret Service's interest in the organization were definitely weighing heavily in his considerations.

As clearly as if Belle had read the words on his face, she knew that Opal had reached his decision.

Even as the juggler rose from his seat on the table, the door of the dressing room opened!

Because the door swung inward, Belle could not see the new arrival from where she was sitting. With a cold, sickening feeling assailing her, she assumed that O'Reilly, or another member of the organization, had appeared on the scene. Confronted by another conspirator, Opal might decide that discretion was the better part of valor. Especially as he could, if he had decided on the financial benefits of a betrayal, contact another member of the Secret Service without any great difficulty.

Then Belle became aware of how Opal was reacting.

"That didn't ta—" the juggler began, glancing at the doorway. Starting to bring his gaze back in Belle's direction, he snapped it rapidly toward the door once more, in what would one day be called a "double-take." "Wha—Where—"

The man framed in the doorway was not O'Reilly. Tilted at a jaunty angle, a black stovepipe hat topped a thatch of longish flaming-red hair. He was tall, well built. Almost V-shaped rufous brows grew thickly above deep-set eyes, a hooked nose, tight lips, and a sharp chin. There was something sinisterly Mephistophelian about him, accentuated by his scarlet-lined black opera cloak and matching broadcloth coat, vest, and trousers. His white shirt had wide, hard-starched detachable cuffs, a celluloid collar, and a black silk cravat knotted in the manner of a bow tie.

"Hello Dexter," the newcomer greeted. "They said at your rooming house that I'd find you here. I've been waiting all day to get a chance to talk with you in private. I suppose you remember me?"

"M-Mephisto!" Opal croaked, staring in fascination at the speaker. "I—I heard you were d-dead."

"The report was premature," the man replied, having glanced about him as if to make sure that they were alone in the theater. He advanced into the room. "Although I was close—"

Realizing that the newcomer was not O'Reilly, nor—if Opal's reactions were anything to go on—another member of the organization, Belle twisted on her rump and kicked the door closed. That achieved the desired effect of bringing the man's attention in her direction. At first he seemed to be on the point of defending himself. Then, as his eyes roamed over her and took in her bound wrists, a smile of understanding flickered to his lips.

"What's this, Dexter?" the man inquired sardonically, returning his gaze to the juggler. Taking off his hat with the left hand, he held it so that the right was just inside its mouth. "Don't tell me you've started playing your little games with *girls* now?"

"What do you want here, Mephisto?" Opal challenged.

"Information," the man replied. "I'm looking for good old Simmy Lampart. Where is he?"

"How would I know?" Opal demanded, then went on just a shade too quickly. "I did hear that he's gone to Mexico."

"He's not there, and you know it," Mephisto growled. "Come on, Dexter, tell me where I can find him and I'll leave you to go on playing bound-and-gagged with the lady."

"I don't know how true it is," Opal said, spitting out the words like an alley cat faced by a hound dog, "but I did hear he's founded a town for outlaws somewhere in the wilds of Texas."

"So that's what you heard, is it?" Mephisto purred.

"A dancing boy I know met an outlaw called Joey Pinter who'd been there," Opal elaborated, raising the Derringer to line it on his visitor's chest. "He said Simmy and Giselle do their magic tricks to entertain the Indians. You know, their sawing-the-woman-in-half routine. Now get going!"

"You're sure it was them?"

"The descriptions fitted them. Now go. I've done all I can for you."

While the men had been talking, Belle had taken the opportunity to adopt a posture which would permit a great freedom of movement. Easing herself upward, she halted, kneeling on her bent right leg and with her left foot braced against the wall, to be used as a spring that would propel her erect in a hurry when the time came. She also studied the newcomer and drew certain conclusions. That mop of red hair was a wig and his face . . .

"It's not quite that easy," Mephisto explained with disarming pleasantness, ignoring the Derringer's .41-caliber superposed tubes. He dropped the hat, and his left hand rose to rub at the underside of his jaw. "You see, Simmy is another who thinks I'm dead—"

"So?" Opal challenged.

"So *you* know I'm alive and you always were a blabber-mouth," Mephisto replied. "I'd hate for anything to disillusion Simmy about me."

With that, the man twisted his extended right arm and a bunch of brightly colored paper flowers materialized—apparently from thin air—in his hand. At the same instant, his left fingers hooked under and seemed to rip all the skin and hair from his head.

Removing what Belle had suspected was a cleverly constructed mask, the man exposed what lay underneath.

There was no face as such!

Only a hideous mass of cratered, seamed, dirty-gray flesh without any real semblance of a nose or lips; but from which glowed deep, burning, hate-filled eyes.

# 7
# YOU'RE NOT MUCH BETTER OFF

Letting out a strangled, horrified gasp, Opal swung his head away from the ghastly sight presented by Mephisto. Down whipped the scar-faced man's left hand. Still clasping the mask and wig—which looked like a grotesque, bloodless scalp removed by an Indian warrior—he struck the top of Opal's extended right wrist with some force. The Remington slipped from the juggler's limp fingers, and he involuntarily stumbled back a couple of steps.

Up and across whipped Mephisto's right hand. The lamp's light flickered briefly on something which gave off a metallic gleam among the paper blossoms. Their heads passed beneath Opal's chin and jerked sideways. A momentary shocked and pained expression twisted at the juggler's features. Blood gushed thickly from a gash, which laid open his throat almost to the bone, in the wake of the moving flowers. Gagging out strangled, meaningless words, Opal twisted around and stumbled blindly across the room. With hands clawing unavailingly at the terrible mortal wound, he collapsed against the wall and slid to the floor.

Although the sight of Mephisto's ravaged features, taken with the expression on Opal's stricken face, almost nauseated Belle, she forced herself to remain calm. To give way to panic, or "go woman"—as the Rio Hondo gun wizard,

Dusty Fog,* had once referred to becoming hysterical—
might easily prove fatal. She would need every ounce of
her courage, and to keep her wits about her, if she hoped
to survive.

"Th-thanks, mister," she said, staying in her crouching
posture and contriving to sound grateful. "I think he was
planning to kill me."

"Was he?" Mephisto replied, moving forward with the
bloody blade of the razor-sharp spear-pointed knife seeming almost incongruous in its surrounding of gore-sod-
dened paper flowers. "Then you're not much better off."

Belle did not need an explanation of what he was implying. Having seen him commit a cold-blooded murder, she
could make an excellent witness for the peace officers who
would investigate his crime.

Studiously avoiding looking at Mephisto's face, Belle
concentrated upon watching his right hand. He lunged forward, directing his thrust towards her torso. It was the
swift, deadly efficient attack of a trained knife fighter.

Instinctively, almost without the need for conscious
thought, Belle's savate training had supplied a possible solution to her predicament. Thrusting with her left foot and
straightening her right knee, she rose swiftly. Using the
momentum of her rising, she brought up her left leg and
swung it in a circular motion. The inside edge of her left
boot struck the man's arm at the elbow before the knife
reached her. Such was the power of the kick that it not
only deflected the blade, but also caused his upper body to
turn away from her.

Lowering her foot, Belle ducked her right shoulder and
charged. She rammed into Mephisto's back before he had
recovered from her kick. Dropping his mask, wig, and
weapon, he went reeling away from her. Colliding with the
dressing table, he sent the lamp flying and rebounded at an

* Details of Belle's association with Dusty Fog are given in The Colt and the
Sabre, The Rebel Spy, The Hooded Riders, and The Bad Bunch.

angle. His progress was halted when he ran up against the corner of Opal's trunk. Falling to the floor, the lamp broke and its fuel burst into flames.

Staggering slightly from the impact, Belle managed to regain control of her movements. Then she made preparations to defend herself even more effectively. Darting to where the Remington pistol lay, she grabbed for it. Having her wrists lashed together did not prevent her from retrieving the weapon—although she moved more clumsily than would have been the case if she was free. Her fingers curled around the Derringer's "bird's head" handle. Hooking her thumb over the hammer, she eased it back to full cock—a precaution which Opal had failed to take. Holding the weapon, she swiveled, dropping into a crouching position, ready to start shooting.

Having lost his disguised knife, and realizing that the girl was not acting in blind panic, Mephisto sought for some other means of protecting himself. His eyes flickered to where the flames were licking up the wall and spreading from the shattered lamp. Snatching up Belle's cloak, he flung it at her. It landed over her head and shoulders, enveloping the Derringer as it slanted in his direction.

Belle flung herself to the wall, fighting to throw off the cloak. Instead of following her, Mephisto bounded to and snatched up his mask, wig, and hat. He then darted to the door, ignoring the girl. Jerking it open, he plunged out of the room.

Although she dragged away the cloak, Belle continued to grasp it in her left hand. Following Mephisto from the dressing room, she found that he was already well on his way to making good his escape. Before she could do anything constructive, he had gone through the stage door and disappeared into the darkness. Belle did not attempt to follow, knowing that she must leave his capture to the local peace officers.

Turning back, she felt the heat of the growing fire beating at her and gave her attention to Opal. One glance, even across the width of the room, told her that he was beyond human help. Nor, with the way the flames were spreading, could she make a search of his property.

Still clutching the cloak, which she knew that she would need if she hoped to return to her hotel unnoticed, Belle quit the dressing room. She was on her way to the stage door, which Mephisto had left wide open, when a male figure appeared at it. For a moment, she wondered if the scarred man had returned. Then she realized that it was somebody just as dangerous to her well-being.

It was O'Reilly!

What was more, the recognition was mutual!

Letting out a snarling curse, the man sprang forward. His right hand dipped into his jacket pocket and emerged gripping a Colt Cloverleaf House Pistol.*

Encumbered by the cloak, Belle responded in the only way she dared under the circumstances. Raising the Derringer, she found the task easier in that her right hand was supported by the left wrist. Swiftly she took aim, remembering the old Texas axiom that "Speed's fine—but accuracy is final," and shot to kill. A .41 ball spiked between and just over the man's eyes. Spinning around, he let his revolver fall and followed it down.

Running toward the stage door, Belle glanced at O'Reilly and went out. Behind her, the flames were roaring and throwing an eerie red glow from the dressing room's door. She heard yells of alarm and shouts of "Fire!" Remembering that her captors had spoken of other members of the organization being expected at the theater, she did not linger in the hope of obtaining assistance to free her hands. Holding the cloak out to one side, she darted as fast as she could toward an alley between two darkened, empty-looking buildings.

Standing in the shadows of the alley, Belle looked about her and strained her ears to detect any hint of Mephisto's

---

* Despite its name, the Colt Cloverleaf House Pistol is a revolver.

presence. Later she might find time to ponder on the reason for his visit to the theater and wonder if his search for "good old Simmy Lampart" was connected with the hideous damage that had been inflicted upon his face. She would also remember to notify the appropriate authorities about the "town for outlaws" which Lampart was alleged to have founded in the wilds of Texas.*

At that moment, however, Belle's only concern with Mephisto was in locating and dealing with him if he should be lurking in the vicinity.

Satisfied that the strange, terribly scarred man had not lingered after fleeing from the theater, Belle dropped the cloak and tucked the Remington into her waistband. Gratefully, she turned her thoughts to finding the means of escaping from her bonds.

Lifting her wrists, she felt for and gripped the knot with her teeth. The men had improvised, using the silk scarf as being the item most readily available and confident that she could not escape as long as they had kept her under surveillance. Free from such observation, she made short work of the knot, and it yielded to her teeth's tugging. Released from the scarf's clutches, she dropped it with a sigh of relief and retrieved her cloak. Donning it and raising the hood, she peered back in the direction from which she had come.

Although a number of people had gathered at the theater, so far no fire-fighting appliances had arrived. Nor, by the lack of interest displayed in her position, had she been seen as she had taken her departure. Some attempt was being made to deal with the blaze, apparently. Even as Belle watched, two men emerged from the stage door, dragging O'Reilly's lifeless body between them. She wondered what they had made of finding a dead man—shot in the head—inside the burning building.

* The reasons why Mephisto was searching for Simmy Lampart, along with details of "the town for outlaws," are given in Hell in the Palo Duro and Go Back to Hell.

Which raised the matter of what Belle should do next.

The most obvious answer was for her to notify the police of her part in the affair and give them a description of Mephisto.

Unfortunately, in Belle's line of work, the obvious answer was only rarely acceptable.

If she told the authorities her story, they might possibly be able to find and arrest the hideously marked man. On the other hand, it was such an unlikely story that they might not believe her. In either event, time would be wasted while they checked up on her veracity. General Handiman would not be pleased if word leaked out that Belle Boyd, the Rebel Spy, was employed as a member of the United States Secret Service.

There was also another, more immediate aspect to consider before she reported to the civic authorities. A proportion of the police in every large city were Irishmen. Which meant that one of them, already involved in the plot, might hear what she had to say and inform his fellow conspirators.

By returning to the Travelers Hotel immediately, Belle might find the opportunity to search O'Reilly's room. If she should be held by the police and one of them happened to be in league with the conspirators, he could arrange for somebody to anticipate her, visit the dead man's quarters, and remove any evidence.

So Belle knew that she must keep quiet for the time being. Perhaps by doing it, she might allow Mephisto to escape. Nothing she had seen of Opal caused her to regret delaying, possibly even ruining, the peace officers' chances of arresting his murderer.

Having reached her conclusions, Belle put them into practice. Wrapping the cloak tightly about her, she stepped from the alley. If anybody outside the theater noticed her, they did not connect her with the fire. So she returned to the street without being interrupted. Walking along until she saw a one-horse cab, she hailed it and asked to be taken to the Travelers Hotel.

On her arrival at her temporary home, Belle paid off the cab. She entered and crossed the foyer. The desk clerk gave her a cursory glance, then resumed his scrutiny of the newspaper he had been reading. Meeting nobody on the stairs, the girl was delighted to find the second floor's passage equally deserted. She knew the danger of passing up a good opportunity and figured that she had better cash in on it. Although she had not conducted any tests, she felt sure that the hotel's locks would be fitted to handle a master key. If so, she would find no difficulty in gaining access to O'Reilly's room.

Removing the pick from its sheath in her boot, Belle went to work. Her belief was justified by results. Finding the master lever, she unfastened the lock and entered the room. Bolting the door to prevent anybody from coming in and catching her, she made other arrangements for her safety. Crossing to it, she opened the window and placed the rope—secured to a ring in the wall and supplied as a means of escape in case of a fire—ready for tossing out and use if the need arose. Then she increased the flame of the lamp on the dressing table.

Starting with O'Reilly's working clothes, which were on the end of the bed, Belle went through every pocket. Making certain that she left no trace of her examination, she searched his other garments. There was not so much as a scrap of paper to help her. Nothing in the room hinted that O'Reilly, or Sheriff, belonged to an Irish nationalist movement.

Turning from the clothing, Belle extended her efforts to the room. The dressing table's drawers and the bed proved to be as unproductive as his garments. Inside the wardrobe were two carpetbags. Taking one of them up, she was surprised by its weight. So she set it on the floor and opened it, to find it held what looked like two lumps of coal. Puzzled, Belle reached for the larger lump. As soon as she touched it, she sensed that it was something a whole lot more dangerous than coal.

One of the problems which had faced the Confederate States all through the War had been how to counteract the strangling efficiency of the Federal Navy's blockade on Southern ports. To this end, several devices had been manufactured and used with various degrees of success. Among the most novel had been the "coal torpedo."

Simple to produce, effective in operation, the device—it would have been called a booby trap in later years—had been nothing more than a hollow-cast chunk of iron, filled with gunpowder and shaped like a piece of coal. To further disguise its purpose, it had then been coated with tar and coal dust. The idea behind the deception was that, when left by Confederate agents in Union marine fuel depots, the torpedoes would be taken aboard Yankee warships. When a torpedo was fed into a furnace by a stoker, it exploded and blew up the boilers. Belle knew that at least three Northern vessels had been set on fire and destroyed in such a manner.

What Belle could not understand was why O'Reilly would have the coal torpedoes in his baggage. Great Britain had the most powerful navy in the world, so they might be intended as a means of dealing with blockading warships. Or they could have some other purpose in the fight to "liberate" Ireland. Maybe the two examples were being sent to show "freedom fighters" in the "ould country" how to produce more of them. Yet Belle thought that the organization ought to be able to find some better way of transporting the samples.

Slowly the girl turned the coal torpedo over in her hands. It looked as if it had been made some time ago. While it was black, all its original coating of tar and coal dust had been removed. That had left a metallic glint which might be noticeable when compared with the genuine article.

Belle wondered where the coal torpedoes had come

from. Possibly they had been part of a consignment overlooked at the end of the War, or kept as mementos. Irishmen had rendered good and loyal service to the Confederate States, and one of them might have had the dangerous
items in his possession or have known how to make them.
If it came to a point, a man with Northern persuasions
might have heard about them and decided to make some
for his own purposes.

Realizing that she had neither the time nor the inclination for idle conjecture, Belle replaced the coal torpedo.
She put the bag back into the wardrobe and ascertained
that its companion was empty. Satisfied that the room held
nothing of interest, she reduced the lamp's glow. Closing
and fastening the window, she went to the door. Opening
it, she stepped out ready to act as if she had been making a
legal visit. She still had the passage to herself, so she
locked the door behind her.

Safely in her own room, Belle removed the cloak. She
studied her reflection in the wardrobe's mirror, touching
her jaw gingerly and wincing a little. After making such
repairs as she felt were necessary to her appearance, she
sat on the bed and gave thought to her next line of action.

Once again Belle was faced with the problem of what to
do for the best.

Should she stay at the hotel and hope that somebody
would come to search O'Reilly's room? Or ought she to go
as arranged to examine the consignment in Molloy's warehouse?

If she took the former alternative, she might be able to
follow whoever arrived when they left and see what developed. A sound and profitable way of spending the rest of
the evening—provided that somebody came and presup-
posing that she could follow him after his departure without being detected or otherwise losing him.

Against that, there might not be an attempt to collect
O'Reilly's belongings that night. Maybe his companions, or
superiors, would not want to take a chance on drawing

further attention to him. The police would be interested in
him already, more so than was comfortable for the organization. Adding a further mystery would not be to the conspirators' advantage.

Could the others rely upon O'Reilly not to be in possession of incriminating documents?

Belle was inclined to believe that they might. From what
she had seen and deduced, O'Reilly was an intelligent man
and might be high in the organization's chain of command.
As such, he would know better than to keep incriminating
papers in a hotel room. The coal torpedoes would mean
little or nothing, and might be ignored as unconventional
but innocuous souvenirs. They might puzzle the police but
would not be connected with the organization.

So the girl would gamble on the attempt not being made
that night.

A fresh, alarming thought gave added strength to her
decision. She had to consider Darren. He might have made
a fool of himself, but it was technically still his case. So he
had the right to know everything that had happened that
evening. There was also another point about him for her to
consider.

Not only was he expecting Belle, but his life might be in
peril.

Everything depended upon the conclusions drawn by the
conspirators regarding O'Reilly's killing. If they decided
that Darren had been fooling them and was not their dupe,
they could figure on closing his mouth. Despite the prominent manner in which he displayed his gun—or rather because of it—Belle doubted if Darren would be capable of
protecting himself against an unexpected attack.

What was even worse from Belle's point of view, she
could indirectly contribute to Darren's being taken un-
awares. Hearing a knock at his door and expecting her to
arrive, he was likely to open up without first checking who
might be at the other side. Belle might dislike Darren, but
she had no desire to have his death on her conscience.

Replacing the cloak, Belle hurried down to the foyer and asked the desk clerk to find her a cab. If he was puzzled by her second departure, the man concealed it very well. Leaving the desk, he carried out her request. While he was gone, Belle wondered if she might confuse a possible visitor to O'Reilly's quarters. She remembered hearing of how a professional gambler of her acquaintance had saved his life by altering the number of his hotel room.* However, she decided against making such an attempt. Probably whoever came would know in which room O'Reilly had been lodging, and so would be suspicious if he checked and found an alteration in the register.

Boarding the cab, Belle told its driver to go to the street upon which the warehouse and Darren's hotel were situated. While being carried in the required direction, she felt the uneasy sensation rising again. Somehow, she was certain that there were ramifications to the affair which had not yet fully come to her attention.

* *Told in* Cold Deck, Hot Lead.

# 8

# THE SHIPMENT'S GOING
# ON SATURDAY

"Hello, Miss Boyd," Darren greeted, having opened the door without checking who was at it. However, he stood with his right hand concealed, and she guessed that it held his revolver. She also figured that the weapon was there merely to impress her with his preparedness. "I'd almost given you up."

"I had a little difficulty getting here," Belle replied, walking by him.

Having left the cab some distance from the hotel, Belle had continued the journey on foot. She had kept a keen watch for anybody who might have had the building under observation, but felt sure that no one was present. The hotel did not maintain a permanently manned desk, so she had gone unchallenged on her arrival. At Darren's door, she had paused and steeled herself against the possibility of having reached him too late. It had been a relief when he had opened up to her knock.

Watching Darren twirl the bulky, short-barreled British Webley Bulldog revolver on his forefinger, as a preliminary to tucking it under his waistband, Belle could hardly hold down her smile. There was no wonder that the Irishman had become suspicious of him. However, he had shown sufficient good sense to dress suitably for the expedition.

The clothes he had worn earlier were replaced by a black shirt, matching trousers, and Indian moccasins.

"What kind of trouble?" Darren inquired, then remembered his duties as a host. "Let me take your cloak."

On removing and handing over the cloak, Belle saw surprise and then grudging approval flicker across Darren's face. He laid the cloak on the bed and indicated a chair at the table.

"Did you see the fire at the Bijou Theater?" Belle asked, sitting down.

"Is that where it was? I saw the glow and heard the commotion. By the way, O'Reilly said that the shipment's going on Saturday."

In his eagerness to pass on the choice tidbit of information, Darren was clearly dismissing the fire at the theater and Belle's difficulties as of minor consideration. He searched her face for some hint that she was overawed by his words. Nothing showed. In fact she appeared to be taking it very casually.

"How did you come to meet him?" Belle wanted to know.

"In the saloon along the street," Darren replied. "Not that I make a habit of going into saloons when I'm working—"

"It's lucky that you broke your rule. But *how* did you get to know him?"

"Luck, mostly. He was cursing Molloy for a Protestant son of a bi—Well, I could see that he didn't like Molloy. You know how Irish Catholics are where the Protestants are concerned?"

"I've heard about it," Belle admitted, but the full significance of the words did not register at that moment. She was to remember them later. "So you made him an offer to spy on Molloy?"

"It took a little longer than that," Darren protested. "But that's about how it happened. He's been very useful."

"I'm sure he has. Where does he live?"

"I couldn't say for sure. Nor far away, most likely."

"At the Travelers Hotel?"

"That's not likely," Darren stated. "It would be too expensive for him."

"I'd have thought that," Belle remarked. "Except that I followed him there after he left you."

"He must have been delivering a message or something!" Darren insisted. "On his pay, he couldn't afford to live there."

"Not on a warehouse hand's pay, I agree," Belle drawled. "But he's been there since the day the consignment reached Memphis. Claiming to be a Pinkerton detective, Sheriff by name."

"How did the Pink-eyes* get involved?" Darren asked dazedly. Then a glint of understanding showed. "I suppose they're on to this affair and are trying to show they're more efficient than the Secret Service, as usual."

Ever since Allan Pinkerton had retired from the Secret Service at the end of the War and had resumed operations with his National Detective Agency, there had been considerable rivalry between the two organizations. Members of the Secret Service believed, possibly without justification, that the Pinkerton family would not be averse to seeing them fail in their appointed duties—and for Congress to be compelled to turn to the National Detective Agency for assistance.

"I'd be surprised if O'Reilly really was a Pink-eye," Belle stated. "That was just an excuse he used at the hotel, so that he could come and go in his working clothes without arousing comment."

Watching Darren's face start to register alarm and realization, Belle suddenly felt sorry for him. He was young, inexperienced, but desperately eager to make good. Possibly he had never received any training for the exacting

---

* Pink-eye: derogatory name for a member of the Pinkerton National Detective Agency.

work in which he was engaged. Trying to break her news as gently as possible to him, she went on to describe all that had happened since she had left him.

"You went alone?" Darren growled, when Belle reached the point where she had broken into the theater.

"Everybody makes mistakes," Belle answered, with an attitude of apology that she did not feel. "I believed that I could take him prisoner—"

"You?"

"I'm an expert at savate; and I expected to have the element of surprise in my favor."

"Yes, but—"

"It *was* a mistake," Belle conceded. "But *all* of us make them. Don't *we?*"

"Yours could have gotten you killed," Darren warned, taking the point.

"It nearly did," Belle admitted wryly, touching her jaw. Continuing with her story, she concluded by saying, "Neither Opal nor O'Reilly was Irish."

"O'Reilly always sounded like a Mick-lander to me," Darren protested.

"Not when he was speaking to Opal. He was a Southron then," Belle countered. "Of course, he would probably have put on an Irish accent for your benefit."

"How about Opal," Darren inquired, changing the subject. "I've seen him on the stage, but he does a dumb act and I've never heard him speak. Where does he fit into all this?"

"That's puzzling me too. Apparently they were planning to hold a meeting of some kind at the theater tonight—"

"Not *tonight*. Opal had taken over the Bijou to give a show for Confederate veterans. A *free* show, so there'd be a good attendance."

"And provide an excellent excuse for a large number of conspirators to get together. Nobody would notice them, attending a free show at a theater."

"That's true," Darren agreed. "O'Reilly's crowd must

have employed Opal to do just as you say. But he's an important performer. Why would he do it?"

"For money, I'd say," Belle guessed. "It certainly wasn't through patriotism or any other high motive. I'd almost persuaded him to set me free and help us against them, for a price, when Mephisto walked in."

"Who is this Mephisto?" Darren asked.

"A professional magician, or something of the kind, I'd reckon. He must have picked the lock, which wouldn't take a genius. But the way he produced the bunch of flowers was no beginner's trick. Opal knew him and seemed surprised to see him, but I don't think he's connected with our business."

"Or me," Darren agreed, showing that he was willing to dismiss Mephisto from his thoughts on those grounds.

"What do we do about him?" Belle demanded.

"Who?"

"Mephisto. He murdered Opal in cold blood."

"For his own private reasons. He's hardly our concern—"

"The hell he isn't!" Belle barked, then felt contrite as she identified the cause of her irritation. "I'm sorry. My conscience is pricking me. If I'd gone straight to the police—"

"They probably wouldn't have caught him. It's not likely he would have stayed around, with people coming from all sides to the fire," Darren consoled her. "Besides, it's possible that Captain O'Shea would be in sympathy with the Irish nationalists, even if he isn't in cahoots with them."

"That's possible," Belle sighed. "In fact, I'd thought of it."

"Anyway, *I* think you acted for the best," Darren declared and put up almost the same reasons that Belle had considered when she was deciding against speaking to the police. "What you could do is write an anonymous letter describing this Mephisto and pretending that he killed Opal and O'Reilly while trying to rob the theater. That way, O'Shea's men will know who to look for, and we won't need to become involved."

"That's what I'll do," Belle agreed. "But if O'Shea's with them, it might make them suspicious. That could be dangerous for *you.*"

"We'll worry about that when the time comes," Darren assured her.

"You said that the shipment will be going on Saturday?" Belle prompted, wanting to avoid a demonstration of heroics.

"Yes. They're sending it downriver to New Orleans."

"Why New Orleans?"

"So it can be put on a ship for Ireland," Darren replied. He did not add the words "of course," but they were there.

"They could do that far more easily in New York or any of the East Coast ports," Belle reminded him.

"Which is where we'd expect them to ship from," Darren countered.

"True," Belle conceded. "Only that doesn't explain why O'Reilly should be telling you their plans."

"I'd been paying him for information."

"How well did you pay him?"

"Huh?"

"Have you been paying him enough for him to have been able to move into the Travelers Hotel?" Belle elaborated.

"Of course I hadn't!" Darren snorted indignantly. "Unc—Mr. Stenhouse keeps a sharp eye on my—all his agents' expenditure. I gave O'Reilly five dollars for each report and increased it to twenty for tonight's information."

"That hardly seems enough money to have made him decide to turn traitor," Belle admitted, having withheld any mention of the disparaging comments made by Opal concerning Darren's abilities. "Could they have suspected that you're watching the shipment?"

"I don't see how they could have!"

"And you never let O'Reilly, or anybody else, know that you're a member of the Secret Service?"

"Certainly *not!*" Darren stated vehemently, but his cheeks reddened and he refused to meet her eyes.

"Then it's a mystery," Belle drawled, and let the subject drop.

There was nothing to be gained, other than profitless self-satisfaction, in exposing the young man's inadequacies. Belle knew that she would be working with him, at least until Saturday. Letting him know how badly he had failed would shatter his confidence. It was sure to render him useless for anything that might lie ahead.

Yet, as Belle knew, there were many puzzling aspects to the affair. Time, thought, and investigation would supply the answers. Until then, Darren must be prevented from brooding and, if possible, stopped from drawing the correct conclusions about how he had been fooled by O'Reilly.

"Is everything ready for our visit to the warehouse?" Belle asked.

"Yes," Darren replied. "If you still think it's worth our while going."

"Why wouldn't it be?"

"Well, we know that the shipment's going. So all we need to do is arrest Molloy and his men."

"Which you could have done on the day that it arrived," Belle pointed out.

"It wouldn't have got us anywhere then," Darren objected.

"Nor will it now," Belle replied. "We'd pick up a few men, with little real evidence against them, and the remainder of the organization will go free to make fresh arrangements."

"Then what do you suggest?" Darren demanded.

"Do you know how the shipment is going to be carried out?"

"On the *Prairie Belle*—"

"Fortune still favors the fair!" Belle exclaimed.

"Huh?" grunted the puzzled male agent.

"Nothing," Belle smiled. "Go on."

"I don't know any more. Except that it's to be held in Rattigan's warehouse until it's collected, just like here," Darren responded. Then an idea struck him. "Hey though! If they were suspicious, he might have told me that to mislead me. Now they're counting on me relaxing. Then they'll move it earlier."

"That's possible," Belle agreed, having reached a similar conclusion. "They might even be planning to move it tonight. The sooner we've taken a look at that consignment, the easier I'll be."

"I've got the ladder, a bull's-eye lantern—"

"We won't need the ladder, given luck," Belle interrupted. "It's too early for that. Besides, Mephisto isn't the only one who can pick locks."

Although he looked a little skeptical, Darren allowed Belle to have her way. Lighting his bull's-eye lantern, he escorted the girl from the hotel and learned some of the basic precautions to take when embarking upon such a mission. Not until Belle had checked on the street did she permit them to emerge. Next, she insisted that they take an indirect route to the warehouse. Reaching its left side door, she breathed a silent prayer that she could manipulate the lock. If she failed, the respect with which Darren was now regarding her would rapidly diminish.

Holding his Webley, the young man kept guard while Belle manipulated her pick. The lock was not equipped with a master lever, but she managed to align and operate the other plates.

"Neatly done, Miss Boyd!" Darren enthused, as the lock clicked and Belle eased open the door.

"Thank you," the girl answered, stepping into the gloomy building.

"The boxes are across this way," Darren advised, opening the front of his lantern as he followed Belle inside. "I'll—"

"Let me lock the door first!" Belle ordered, closing it hurriedly. "Somebody just might happen by and try the handle."

Instead of debating the matter, as would have happened earlier in their acquaintance, Darren yielded to greater experience. Still grasping the Webley in his right hand, he waited until Belle had relocked the door. Then they crossed the room to the consignment.

"There's no hope of opening these," Belle commented, indicating the firmly nailed lids of the rifle and ammunition boxes. She took hold of the rope carrying handle of an oblong box and lifted to test the weight. "But they seem to be all right."

"Why shouldn't they be?" Darren demanded.

"No reason at all," Belle answered, although she could think of at least one very good reason. "Can you put the light on the bales, please?"

"There's no doubting what's in *them,*" the young man replied, doing as she had requested. He illuminated one of the bales. "This has uniforms in it. There's a tear in the covering, and you can see the buttons on a jacket. If you feel at the next, you can make out the shape of boots. The one with the hats has a rip in it too. Not a big one, but it lets you see some of the brims. They're tucked one into another, you know."

"Huh-huh!" Belle grunted, bending closer to scrutinize the tear and the brass military buttons on a dark blue background. From them, she made a close study of the bale's edges.

"All of them have been opened and stitched again," Darren informed her. "The two men would have had that done so they could examine the contents before making the purchase."

"Yes," Belle agreed. "Shall we go?"

"We may as well," Darren affirmed, but his attitude

stated that he believed they should never have bothered coming. "What did you expect to find?"

"Not a thing," Belle sighed and returned toward the door through which they had made their entrance. "Kill that light!"

"Wha—" Darren began, but obeyed. "What is it?"

Aware of the necessity for unceasing alertness when on such a mission, Belle had constantly darted glances at the building's various windows. So she had observed a light through the one nearest to the left-hand door. People were approaching, one of them carrying a lantern. Faintly, the sound of the words still inaudible, voices reached the intruders' ears. However, Belle did not notice any change in the timbre to suggest that they had seen the faint glow from Darren's bull's-eye lantern.

"What're we going to do?" Darren hissed, and Belle could sense that his gun hand was quivering with eagerness.

"Stand one on each side of the door and wait," Belle replied. "If they come in, we'll jump them. Don't speak; crack your man on the head with your gun."

"No shooting?" Darren whispered.

"Only if there's no other way of doing it," Belle replied. "There're only two of them, but others might be close by."

"Or they could just be passing on their way home," Darren sniffed.

Once again, the young man proved to be a poor judge of a situation. Nearer came the two men and their voices preceded them. By now, Belle and Darren could hear what was being said.

"What do you reckon come off at the theater, Mick?" one of the pair was saying in a deep local accent.

"Sure, and Gaylorne must've been riling that swish* again," replied the other. He at least sounded Irish. "Opal

* *Swish: derogatory name for a male homosexual.*

never took to it. Maybe they had a fight, the lamp got knocked over, and they shot each other."

"Opal wouldn't've dared start anything," the first man protested.

"Some of those swishes can get mean, you rile them enough," Mick insisted. "Way his body looked when they got the fire out, we'll never know if I'm right."

"The Frenchman wasn't any too pleased about it. I'm not sorry he'll be going down the river tomorrow. He's a bad bastard when anything crosses him."

"He got crossed tonight," Mick commented. "That fire ruined his meeting."

"You sound as if that pleases you."

"It does, Andy-darlin'. We're not ready for anything as open as that yet."

"I dunno," Andy replied, halting at the door. "It wasn't going to be like it will in Shreveport."

"What'll happen there?" Mick inquired. "Hey! What're you doing?"

"Like Molloy said. Going in to make sure everything's all right."

"Why bother? That damned knobhead at the hotel couldn't've gotten in. He only made it last time because we left the door in the hayloft unlocked. Anyway, if he gets in, there's nothing for him to see."

"Nothing he hasn't already seen," Andy admitted. "You know, Mick, there's a feller who's lucky to be alive. When the Frenchman heard he was following the stuff, his first thought was to kill the bastard, as painfully as possible. He'd have done it too, but for Gaylorne saying we could make use of such a stupid son of a bitch."

Standing in the darkness, Belle could hear Darren breathing more quickly. Clearly he knew that he was the "stupid son of a bitch" in question. Maybe he was even aware that, in range-country parlance, a "knobhead" was an exceptionally stupid, worthless mule. Certainly he must be boiling with rage and mortification at having his faults discussed in such detail. Belle hoped that he would control his temper and not disclose their position prematurely.

There was a faint scrabbling sound close to Belle's hand, then the lock clicked.

Crouching slightly in the stygian blackness, Belle prepared to launch a devastatingly effective savate attack upon one of the men as they entered. She hoped that she could rely on Darren to deal with the other. Easing back silently, she avoided being caught in the pool of light which followed the opening of the door.

"Aw, the hell with it, Andy," Mick said, before either of them had stepped inside. "Why bother? He couldn't get in and won't want to anyway, after Gaylorne's told him we're moving the shipment this Saturday. I see more than enough of this place during the day, without going in on my own time."

"And me," Andy admitted, reversing the direction in which the door was moving. "Let's go have a drink, then head back and say everything's fine. Hey though! I wonder who'll get to go now Gaylorne's dead?"

"So do I," Mick agreed, while Andy locked the door and removed the key. "If they was to ask for volunteers, 'tis myself who'd offer. I'd fancy a trip down to New Orleans."

"So would I," Andy drawled. "Even if I did have to finish it riding in Tully Bascoll's boat. Come on. I'll let you buy me a drink."

"Sure, and 'tis kindness itself you are to me, sir," Mick replied. "And I'm thinking it's not the likes of us who'll be getting that ride on the *Prairie Belle.*"

"I'm with you on that," Andy was saying as they strolled away. "But it'd sure be a sight to see, when it happens."

Whatever Mick replied was lost as distance killed the sound of their voices.

# 9
## YOU LOUSY TRAITOR

Twirling her parasol jauntily, as it rested on her left shoulder, Belle Boyd strolled along the wooden dock toward the *Prairie Belle*. It was Friday afternoon and she was going to renew an acquaintance with an old and trusted friend. She was no longer the "Miss Winslow," who had a stateroom on the *Elegant Lady* and patronized the expensive Travelers Hotel. In fact, a lady of "Miss Winslow's" class would probably have drawn aside rather than come into contact with a girl such as Belle appeared to be.

After Andy and Mick had taken their departure from Molloy's warehouse, Belle had faced the task of restoring at least a part of Darren's shattered confidence. Using tact, a little flattery, and some good, sound common sense, she had convinced him that things were not so bad as they appeared. While he had made a few mistakes, Belle had insisted that he could redeem himself if he tried. Such had been her powers of persuasion that she had dragged him from the morass of self-criticism into which he was sinking.

Satisfied that, with Belle's guidance, he could make good, Darren had given her some interesting information. Clearly the organization had wondered if he might have been responsible for the incident at the Bijou Theater. That had been proven by the fact that they had checked up on him. Although Darren had neglected to mention it earlier, he had had a visitor before Belle had arrived. Dressed in the manner of a professional gambler, the man had claimed he was looking for a high-stake poker game and had come to the wrong address. Fortunately, Darren had been in the process of changing his clothes. So he had answered the door in his stocking-feet, gray trousers, no jacket, and a collarless white shirt.

Darren had not only given Belle a good description of his visitor, but—on meeting her at Stenhouse's hotel suite the following morning—had presented her with a sketch of the "gambler's" face.

On hearing of Belle's single-handed visit to the Bijou Theater, Stenhouse had grudgingly admitted that she had acted in the only way possible under the circumstances. He had been less in favor of the Mephisto aspect of the affair. However, he had finally stated that Belle had been correct in her decisions. Promising that he would arrange delivery for the anonymous information and try to learn from the police of any further developments, he had hinted that that side of their business was closed.

Referring to the meeting which Belle had heard her captors discussing, Stenhouse had claimed that it was unlikely to have taken place. Nor, in his opinion, would it have been of any great significance. Probably, he had said, it was no more than a means of raising funds to finance the proposed rebellion. Having no evidence to the contrary, Belle had been inclined to agree with Stenhouse.

There had been a variance of opinion regarding O'Reilly's motives in informing Darren of the shipment's departure. Taking the obvious line, Stenhouse had declared that it would be removed secretly before Saturday. Showing more imagination than previously, Darren had suggested that the organization—having discovered that they were under surveillance by the Secret Service—might be willing to sacrifice the consignment. In doing so, they could be hoping to divert attention from other supplies already in transit or awaiting shipment.

Remembering the conversation which she had overheard at the warehouse, Belle had proposed that O'Reilly had been lying about the means of removal and destination. Perhaps the consignment would be placed on board the *Prairie Belle* but unloaded at some point before New Orleans. After which, it would be transferred to some other, unsuspected boat to complete the delivery.

Realizing the futility of continuing to debate the probabilities, they had turned to deciding what action they should take. For once, Belle had found herself in complete agreement with Stenhouse. There was insufficient evidence to arrest Molloy and his employees. Nor would anything of importance be gained by having the consignment confiscated. The organization would only obtain more arms and continue their operations. To prevent this, they must lay hands on the leaders and organizers. With that in mind, Stenhouse had ruled that the shipment must be allowed to depart. Then Belle and Darren could follow it and, it was hoped, bring about the desired result.

They had also decided that Darren should, in fact must, continue with his established routine and behave as if he was unaware of O'Reilly's death. So he would have to avoid displaying any interest, or surprise, over his "informer's" nonappearance until Friday at the earliest.

With the possibility of the shipment being moved before Saturday, it had been considered advisable that Belle should move into a vacant room at Darren's hotel. She would then be able to help him maintain a constant watch on the warehouse. That had meant she was compelled to purchase suitable clothing to let her blend into the neighborhood.

Before concluding the meeting, they had examined the coverage given in Thursday's copy of the *Memphis Clarion* to the previous night's fire at the Bijou Theater. There had been a brief sketch of Opal's career—the kind of thing he

# ALL YOURS FREE!

**ONE DOZEN BEAUTIFUL FOUR-COLOR
SCENES FROM THE OLD WEST IN THE**

# LOUIS L'AMOUR
# WALL CALENDAR

**(An $8.99 value in stores)**

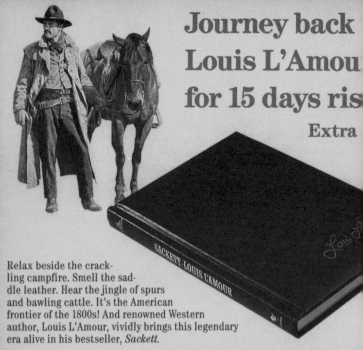

# Journey back
# Louis L'Amou
# for 15 days ris

**Extra**

Relax beside the crackling campfire. Smell the saddle leather. Hear the jingle of spurs and bawling cattle. It's the American frontier of the 1800s! And renowned Western author, Louis L'Amour, vividly brings this legendary era alive in his bestseller, *Sackett*.

Ride into the high country with young Tell Sackett. Follow him into a hidden canyon where he discovers a lost gold mine. It's going to be his secret stake. But the secret doesn't last for long. When Tell and the beautiful Kerry Ange return to the mine, they're trapped by a lawless gang of desperadoes who aim to take the gold and leave no witnesses. If you love action-packed adventure . . .

. . . if the romance of the frontier stirs you . . . if stories that spring from real life appeal to you—you will love *Sackett*. It's a fabulous read and an ideal introduction to the best-selling novels in *The Louis L'Amour Collection!* See for yourself. Preview *Sackett* in a handsomely crafted hardcover Collector's Edition at your leisure for 15 days risk-free.

## SAVE OVER HALF OFF!

If you enjoy *Sackett* as much as I know you will and decide to keep it, simply honor our invoice for only $4.95—*A SAVINGS OF OVER HALF OFF* the current low regular rate of $11.95—plus shipping and handling, and sales tax in NY and Canada, as your introduction to *The Collection* under the terms on the post card at the right.

As soon as we hear from you, your full-color Louis L'Amour Wall Calendar will be on its way—yours to keep absolutely *FREE*. You can't miss! Act now to claim your *FREE GIFT* and *RISK-FREE PREVIEW*!

e Old West with
mpelling novel, *Sackett,*
e!

: You may keep *Sackett* for only $4.95!*

*plus shipping and handling, and sales tax in NY and Canada.

# In Addition to the Free Louis L'Amour Calendar

. . . your risk-free preview volume of *Sackett* will introduce you to these outstanding qualities of the bookbinder's art—

- Each volume is bound in rich, rugged sierra-brown simulated leather.
- The bindings are sewn, not just glued, to last a lifetime. And the pages are printed on high-quality paper that is acid-free and will not yellow with age.
- The title and Louis L'Amour's signature are golden embossed on the spine and front cover of each volume.

would probably have given to a reporter on his arrival. Mention had been made of the disappointment experienced by the Confederate veterans who would have been his guests at the free performance he had arranged for them.

Captain O'Shea of the Memphis Police Department had personally assumed control of the investigation. He had deduced that Opal had been attacked by an unknown man. During the struggle, the lamp in the dressing room had been broken and set on fire. Although the juggler had followed his assailant and killed the man, he had returned to the blazing room—presumably to save his property—and had been overcome by the smoke. The charred condition of Opal's body, when it had been recovered, had precluded any hope of discovering if he had suffered injuries which had contributed to his death.

There had then followed a comment which might have given Belle a clue if she had been in possession of other facts. Discussing motives for the "mystery man's" attack on Opal, O'Shea had "not ruled out the possibility of a pro-Union fanatic resenting the juggler's giving a free performance to entertain ex-members of the Confederate States Navy and Army.

Having been working west of the Mississippi River for some months, the girl had lost touch with conditions in the Southern states. While Stenhouse might have enlightened her, he had failed to do so. In fact, when she had remarked upon O'Shea's statement, he had dismissed it as ill-advised but unimportant and had said pointedly that it was inadvisable to leave the warehouse unobserved for too great a length of time.

Taking the hint, Belle and Darren had left to continue their duties. The day and night had passed uneventfully, and Friday morning had disclosed that the boxes were still in the warehouse. At noon, while Belle kept a watch from her room, Darren had visited the saloon in which he had made O'Reilly's acquaintance. He had been told by a man

—who he had suspected was "Mick," from the night visit to the consignment—that O'Reilly was ill and would not be back at work until Monday morning.

So, as there had been no further developments, Belle had decided to visit the *Prairie Belle*. Unless there had been a drastic change in the crew, she hoped to discover whether or not the consignment would be traveling on the boat.

To conceal her hair and avoid having to use the inappropriate wig, she wore a cheap white "spoon bonnet" which covered her head and looked vaguely like the rear canopy on a Conestoga "prairie schooner" wagon. Although old-fashioned, it was in keeping with her appearance of being a "lady of easy virtue." So was the form-hugging, sleeveless white blouse's extreme décolletage, the cheap, flashy jewelry she sported, and the tight, glossy purple skirt which emphasized the contours of her hips.

Passing among the inevitable crowd of loafers on the dock, Belle felt sure that she was creating the desired impression. Nor, unless the man she had come to meet had changed his ways considerably, would her visit appear to be out of the ordinary.

Having come in at noon, the *Prairie Belle* was a hive of industry. The passengers had disembarked, but at the bows a steady stream of Negro roustabouts trotted along the stage-planks carrying cargo or returning for further loads. They were urged on by a bull-voiced, burly white mate who exhorted, praised, insulted, but never really abused them. In fact, one formed the impression that the roustabouts were enjoying his efforts as much as the listening onlookers. That figured, for the *Prairie Belle* had always had the reputation of being a happy ship.

Reaching the front of the crowd, twirling her parasol and swinging a cheap vanity bag from her other wrist, Belle saw a familiar face. A tall, well-built, good-looking young Negro, better dressed than the roustabouts, stood watching them work with the air of one who had already completed his daily grind.

"Hi there, Willie," Belle greeted, approaching the Negro and hoping that he would not betray her identity. "Where'd I find Mr. Bludso?"

Before the Negro could reply, Belle sensed that somebody had moved to her side. A hand caught hold of her arm in a firm, hard grip.

"Now, what'd a pretty gal like you want with the likes of Jim Bludso?" demanded a hard, tough male voice.

Turning her head, the girl looked into a surly, bristle-covered face under a peaked dark blue hat. Her accoster was a big, thickset man, wearing a blue civilian uniform coat, black trousers, and heavy Wellington leg boots. His appearance matched his voice, hard and tough. From his right wrist dangled a length of stout knotted rope, like the "starter" once used as a means of inflicting punishment by petty officers aboard ships.

"That's my business, bucko," Belle answered, sounding as coarse as she looked. "So get your cotton-picking hands off me."

"I'd do it, was I you, Cap'n Bascoll," the Negro advised politely.

"Who the hell asked you to butt in, shine-boy?" Bascoll demanded, still holding Belle's arm. "On the *Stream Queen*, we keeps the niggers in their place. Don't we, Mr. Tyrone?"

The man to whom the words had been directed moved forward. Big, burly, he had a typically Irish cast of features. Dressed in a similar, if cheaper, manner to Bascoll, he had a heavy riding quirt grasped in his right fist.

"That we do, Cap'n," Tyrone confirmed. "Same as should be done on the *Prairie Belle*."

"I ain't looking for fuss with you gentlemen," Willie said quietly, glancing from the *Stream Queen*'s captain to its mate.

"You ain't knowing your place either," Tyrone warned,

hefting his quirt and striding forward. "But we know how to treat uppity niggers on the *Stream Queen*."

Watching Willie clench his fists, Belle prepared to help him. To do so might draw unwanted attention her way, but she had no intention of allowing him to be assaulted on her behalf. The question was how to do it without attracting too much notice by virtue of her fighting abilities. Luckily, a "lady of easy virtue" could be expected to know a few defensive and offensive tricks.

The need for Belle's intervention did not arise.

Before Belle could move, she saw something hurtling through the air from the direction of the cordwood stacked ready to feed the furnaces on the *Prairie Belle*'s main deck. On striking and enfolding Tyrone's face, the missile proved to be a piece of oil-dripping rag. It had been flung, with considerable precision and accuracy, by the man Belle had come to see.

Bareheaded, with crinkly reddish hair, Jim Bludso—senior engineer of the *Prairie Belle*—was ruggedly good looking. He was tall and powerfully built, yet neither slow nor clumsy. Oil was streaked on his face and the muscular arms that protruded from the rolled-up sleeves of his gray flannel shirt. His black trousers were tucked into Wellington leg boots, and a long-bladed Ames Rifleman's knife hung in a sheath at the left side of his wide waist belt.

Vaulting from the main deck to the dock, Bludso sprang forward. Before Tyrone had managed to claw the oily rag fully from his face, the engineer had come within striking distance.

"You lousy traitor, Bludso!" Bascoll bawled, releasing Belle's arm and lunging in the engineer's direction.

Knotting his right hand into a useful-looking fist, Bludso propelled it solidly against the edge of Tyrone's jaw. The mate pitched sideways, dropping the rag and his quirt, before crashing down and rolling over three times on the hard wooden planks of the dock.

Raising the knotted rope's end, Bascoll intended to lay it

viciously across Bludso's shoulders. Struck there, the engineer would be momentarily incapacitated. Long enough, certainly, for the captain to deliver a more damaging assault with fist or boot.

The treacherous attack was destined never to be completed. Realizing that Bludso might not be able to turn fast enough to cope with his second assailant, Belle took an effective hand. Sliding the parasol through her fingers as she brought it from her shoulder, she grasped its end. Then she reached down, hooking the crook of the handle under Bascoll's rearmost ankle and jerking sharply. Yelling a curse, the captain stumbled. In his efforts to retain his balance, he let the rope's end fly from his fingers.

Turning as fast as a scalded cat, Bludso thrust out his left fist. Hard knuckles collided with Bascoll's nose and halted his advance. A sharp right cross turned it into a retreat. Shooting out first one fist then the other, Bludso drove Bascoll across the dock until the captain was teetering helplessly on the very edge of the planks. Catching hold of the dark blue jacket's breast with his right hand, Bludso restrained Bascoll from tumbling into the water. Then the engineer drew back his left fist.

"Mr. Bludso!" roared a voice from the pilothouse, which perched high on top of the *Prairie Belle*'s upper "texas" deck. "Take your hands off Captain Bascoll immediately!"

"Aye aye, sir!" Bludso replied, having identified the speaker without requiring to look around, and, like any dutiful officer receiving a lawful command from a superior, he obeyed.

Perhaps Bascoll was grateful for the intervention, but it proved to be a mixed blessing. Although Bludso did not deliver another blow to the captain's already bloody and suffering features, he released his grasp on the jacket. Deprived of the engineer's support, Bascoll wailed and plunged almost gracefully backward into the river.

"Behind you, Massa Jim!" Willie yelled.

Watching Bludso, Belle had not troubled to keep Tyrone

under observation. Swinging her gaze in the mate's direction, she decided that Willie's warning was well founded.

Shaking his head from side to side, Tyrone was in a crouching position like a sprinter waiting to start a race. However, his right hand was less innocently occupied. It was reaching toward the quirt which he had earlier discarded. From what Belle saw, the quirt served a second, more deadly purpose than as a mere inducer of recalcitrant horses. The force of its landing had caused the cap of the handle to separate from the remainder. Attached to the cap, and normally concealed inside the quirt, was a razor-sharp knife's blade.

Belle realized that Bludso could not hope to reach Tyrone and prevent him from picking up the knife. So she felt that, being closer, it was up to her to attend to the mate. With that in mind, she darted toward the man.

Reaching the same conclusion as Belle, Bludso did not attempt to advance. Instead, he sent his right hand flashing across to pluck the Ames knife from its sheath. Up, then down whipped his arm. Showing the same precision and aim as when he had flung the oily rag, he sent the weapon spinning through the air. As if drawn by a magnet, its eleven-and-three-quarters-of-an-inch-long blade guided the needle-sharp spear point into Tyrone's right forearm.

Letting out a shriek of anguish, the mate forgot his intention of arming himself. Even as he tried to lurch upright, with his left hand grabbing at the hilt of the Ames knife, he found that he had further troubles coming his way.

Hitching up her skirt and wishing that she had decided to wear her elegant, but stoutly made, Hessian boots, Belle let fly with a kick. She found that she had no need to regret adopting footwear more in keeping with the character she was pretending to be. Her cheap high-buttoned shoes proved adequate for the occasion. Catching Tyrone under the chin with all the power of her slender, yet steel-muscled left leg, she caused his head to snap back. He rose at an increased speed for a few inches, then flopped forward limply. Considering the thud with which he landed, he might have counted himself fortunate that he was unconscious before his body and face struck the timbers.

"Hello, Jim boy," Belle greeted, as the engineer walked toward her. "Remember lil ole me?"

Already Bludso had been studying her in a calculating, yet not too puzzled manner. Recognition, surprise, then understanding flashed briefly across his face to be replaced by a broad grin.

"I surely do, gal," the engineer confirmed, then indicated Tyrone with a jerk of his left thumb. "What's up? Didn't you figure I could handle him?"

"I should have known you could," Belle admitted truthfully, glancing about her to see if any of the onlookers were inclined to take up hostilities on the behalf of Bascoll and Tyrone.

Although Belle failed to locate any further assailants, one of the crowd caught her eye. He was tall, dark, handsome and, if his style of clothing was anything to go by, a successful professional gambler.

That fact alone did not interest the girl.

If the sketch produced by Horatio Darren had been accurate, Belle believed that she was looking at the gambler who had visited the young agent's room on the night of the fire at the Bijou Theater.

# 10

## ARE THEY AFTER YOU OR ME?

"You're lucky we weren't in Helena when you came to the *Belle* asking after me," Jim Bludso remarked, as he and Belle sat at a side table in the almost empty barroom to which he had escorted her. "There's a lil red-haired gal there who'd get into a real tizz happened she'd heard you."

"Knowing you, that could apply in Greenville, Vicksburg, Natchez, and all points down to New Orleans—although maybe not always with a redhead," Belle replied with a smile. "In fact, I nearly didn't chance coming. I was a long time getting over the bruises from the first time we met."

Bludso grinned in sympathy. The incident to which Belle referred had taken place during the War, in New Orleans. On an assignment to smash a Union counterfeiting ring which had operated in that city, Belle had required the services of a safecracker. Because of an incident involving a woman of Bludso's acquaintance, the girl had found herself in a boxing ring and compelled to fight a professional female pugilist.*

"Mind if I ask why you did chance coming?" Bludso drawled. "Not that I'm not real pleased to see you again."

* *Told in* The Rebel Spy.

Before answering, Belle glanced quickly around her.
Apart from the bartender, idly shooting poker dice with a
customer, they had the room to themselves. The two men
were far enough away to be unable to overhear any conversation that took place. So Belle knew that she could supply
her companion with the answer to his question. That was
why they had come to the bar, to talk without the danger of
anybody eavesdropping.

A soaking, furious Captain Bascoll had managed to haul
himself from the river. His appearance on the dock had
coincided with the arrival of a sergeant and a patrolman of
the Memphis Police Department, which had prevented any
further hostilities.

The peace officers had asked questions concerning the
cause of the disturbance, learning that the captain and the
mate of the *Stream Queen* had been the aggressors. On
being asked if he wished to prefer charges, Bludso had
refused to do so. Accepting the decision, the sergeant had
suggested that the two parties stay aboard their respective
vessels and save their feuding until they were long gone out
of his jurisdiction.

Due to being occupied in acting as a witness on Bludso's
behalf, Belle had lost sight of the gambler who had attracted her notice among the crowd. That had meant she
would be unable to satisfy her curiosity about him. So she
had accepted Bludso's offer to go and talk "old times" over
a drink. Belle had wondered if it had been made due to the
engineer's desire to satisfy his curiosity about her presence
on the dock or concerning her appearance. She had settled
on the former reason when Bludso had selected the small
barroom after passing other, better-patronized establish-
ments.

"I need your help, Jim," Belle said frankly.

"You've got it," Bludso promised without hesitation.
"What can I do?"

"Find out if a certain consignment is being sent down to

New Orleans on the *Belle*, and, if it is, arrange for me to travel with you."

"The first's as good as done. Second might take a lil fixing though. We're likely to be running full. So I might not be able to get you a stateroom, unless you'd be willing to share."

"I could share," Belle admitted. "But it might be better if I was alone."

"Huh huh!" Bludso grunted. "We'll go talk to le Verne. He's the clerk and he'll do what he can to help you."

"I'd rather he didn't know who I am," Belle hinted.

"It'll be me that he's doing the favor for," Bludso answered. "Shall we go and see him?"

"Don't you want to know what it's all about?"

"You want help's enough for me. But I figure you'll tell me as much as you can about it."

"I will," Belle agreed. "By the way. Do you ever run across Madame Lucienne when you're in New Orleans?"

"Near enough every trip," Bludso replied and nodded as if he was forming a clearer understanding concerning Belle's activities. "I keep telling her how she's getting too old and fat for *that* game. All it gets me is a hide-blistering. That gal's got an educated tongue."

The few lingering doubts which Belle had harbored faded away with her appreciation of the meaning behind Bludso's words. If Madame Lucienne had let him know that she was now employed by the United States Secret Service, Belle could rely upon his discretion and cooperation.

Recollecting Captain Bascoll's comment, accusing Bludso of being a traitor, Belle decided that the engineer's actions during the War were still misunderstood by some Southrons. Yet she would have imagined that, like her own, Bludso's connections with the Confederate States Secret Service had been made public knowledge. Certainly the term "traitor" struck her as being most inappropriate.

During the War, the original *Prairie Belle* had been sunk

by raiding Yankee gunboats. The crew had escaped and most of them had enlisted in the navy of the Confederate States. Just as loyal as his companions, Bludso had elected to remain in New Orleans. Although he had worked for the Yankees, he had also been a very capable, effective member of Madame Lucienne's spy ring in that city.

Concluding that Bascoll might have employed the term to remind the onlookers of Bludso's supposed treachery during the War—and so to enlist their support or sympathy —Belle put the matter from her thoughts. Holding nothing back, she told the engineer of her current assignment. On hearing that she was dealing with Irish nationalists, Bludso showed what Belle took to be a brief expression of relief. However, it had come and gone again before she could be certain of its existence, to leave his face a mask of interest and understanding.

"So it's the Mick-landers you're after," Bludso drawled quietly at the conclusion of the story.

"Who did you think it might be?" Belle challenged, puzzled by the comment.

"I wasn't sure. You folk handle more'n just spies and trouble-causers, way Lucienne tells it."

"We do. I've been out West hunting counterfeiters for almost a year. And I'm not after any of your friends who might be doing some smuggling."

"As if I'd know folks who'd do that, for shame," Bludso grinned. Then he became serious. "Don't these fellers know what could happen if they go through with their game?"

"I doubt if they'd care, if they do," Belle replied. "Anyway, I have to try and stop them."

"What I don't figure is why that O'Reilly bucko told your man they'd be sending the stuff on the *Belle*," Bludso remarked.

"The way I see it, there are three possibilities," Belle answered. "O'Reilly lied about them sending it on the *Belle*. They are sending it, but not to New Orleans. Or

O'Reilly told the truth for some reason. I like that one least of all."

"We can soon enough check if they're sending it on the *Belle*," Bludso declared, finishing his drink and shoving back his chair. "Le Verne'll tell us that."

"Will I hurt the bartender's feelings if I don't drink this?" Belle inquired, indicating her glass. "One sip was enough for me."

"I surely wouldn't want to hurt his feelings," Bludso grinned, taking and sinking the girl's drink. "After that, even engine oil'll taste good."

Taking Belle on board the boat by the stern stageplank, Bludso led her up the crew's stairs to the boiler or cabin deck. They went along the promenade and entered the big Gentlemen's Cabin section of the saloon. In the small office, next to a bar sufficiently magnificent in appearance that it would not have disgraced the finest saloon in the land, they found Hervey le Verne hard at work. The clerk of the *Prairie Belle*—he would have been called the purser on a seagoing vessel—was a small, birdlike man who conveyed an air of competence.

Setting down a list of supplies that he had been checking, le Verne looked from Bludso to Belle. On the point of returning his gaze to the engineer, the little clerk gave Belle a quick, but more careful scrutiny.

"Well, Jim," le Verne said, lifting his eyes from their examination of the girl's hands. "What can I do for you?"

"Do we have a shipment, four rifle boxes, two ammunition, and four bales aboard this trip?" Bludso asked.

"Not yet. But we should have before sundown."

"Where're we taking it?"

"Right through to New Orleans."

"All the way, huh?" Bludso said.

"I hope so," le Verne replied, his face impassive and almost uninterested apart from his eyes. "It's being stowed right forrard in the hold. That's why it's coming down today."

"Who's sending it, and where to?" Bludso drawled, asking the question that Belle had wanted without the need for prompting.

"The consignors are the Shamrock Supplies Incorporated, although I've never heard of them before," le Verne answered, having checked on the cargo manifest which he plucked from among the other papers on his desk. "The consignee is Rattigan's Warehouse, to await collection. Is that what you want to know?"

"Sure," Bludso agreed. "How're we off for cabin space?"

"Not an empty stall," le Verne declared. "We've one berth, but that's in a gentlemen's stateroom. There might be a vacancy, Miss—"

"Winslow," Belle supplied, smiling.

"There might be a vacancy if you wouldn't object to doubling up with another lady, Miss Winslow."

"We're sure fooling Mr. le Verne, Jim," Belle remarked. "Was it my hands?"

"Partly," the clerk admitted. "Mainly, though, it's part of my duties to separate those who *are* from those who are merely pretending to be."

"Old Hervey knows every gambler, tinhorn, thief, and conjuneero* on the Big Muddy," Bludso praised.

"Not *every* one," the clerk protested good-naturedly.

On an impulse, Belle opened her vanity bag. She had placed Darren's sketch into it before leaving the hotel in the hope that she might see and recognize the gambler. Taking the sketch out, she passed it to the clerk.

"Is this one of those you know?"

"His name's Brunel," le Verne stated. "Is there anything wrong with him?"

"Should there be?" Belle countered.

"I've never seen him before today," the clerk replied. "But he came this afternoon with a letter from a Mr.

---

* Conjuneero: a confidence trickster.

Gaylorne, canceling a booking for a stateroom. Brunel said that he would take it. I agreed. After all, it's not an uncommon thing to happen."

"Looks like he's coming instead of that O'Reilly bucko, Belle," Bludso remarked.

"It does," the girl agreed.

"I won't ask you what this is all about, Miss Winslow," le Verne said soberly. "But I feel I'm entitled to know if this man, or the consignment, will in any way endanger the safety of the *Prairie Belle?*"

"There's no reason that it should," Belle replied. "It's just that my organization is very interested in learning where the consignment is going and who receives it."

"I see," le Verne answered. "Now, with regard to your accommodation—"

"Can you reserve the man's berth, please?" Belle requested. "I'll have a male companion traveling with me."

"Certainly, I'll see to it. But how about you? There might not be a lady's vacancy."

"I could travel as a deck passenger," Belle suggested. "That way, I could keep a closer watch on the consignment."

"That won't be necessary," the clerk objected. "Once it's in the hold, there'll be no way of getting it out before we unload at New Orleans. On top of which, traveling as a deck passenger isn't suitable for a lady."

"It sure as hell isn't," Bludso confirmed thoughtfully.

*"That's* the least of my worries," Belle smiled. "Very few of my kinfolks would regard my line of work as being suitable for a lady."

"We might be able to accommodate you until a stateroom is available," le Verne offered. "There'll be one after Helena."

"I couldn't spend much time on the main deck if I'm traveling as a stateroom passenger," Belle pointed out. "That would draw too much attention to me."

Neither of the men could dispute Belle's point. The

"deck passengers" traveled on the main deck, taking whatever accommodation they could devise, as being the cheapest fare. There was no mingling socially between them and the occupants of the boiler deck's staterooms.

"Couldn't the man—" le Verne began.

"Brunel would recognize him," Belle interrupted. "That's why he's coming, to keep attention from me. Anyway, he wouldn't look the part as a deck passenger."

"There's one way out," Bludso remarked hesitantly. "Happen you're willing to chance it, that is."

"What would it be?" the girl asked.

"Travel down dressed like you are now—and use my cabin."

"You've only got the one bunk in there, Jim," le Verne pointed out.

"I can always bed down by the engines," Bludso countered.

"Would it be out of the ordinary if I did it?" Belle inquired.

"Not especially, except for Jim bedding down by the engines," le Verne answered. "Officers in single cabins are allowed to have their wives along. Some of them even bring *their* wives."

"I'll bet it wouldn't be the first time you've done it, Jim," Belle commented with a smile.

"I'm not married," the engineer protested and looked embarrassed.

"Which doesn't answer my question," Belle remarked. "Seriously though, I think it's a good idea. If I'm traveling as your 'wife,' Jim, I'll be able to come and go with greater freedom than either a deck or a stateroom passenger."

"There would still be the matter of where you both sleep," le Verne warned.

"We'll face up to *that* problem when the time comes," Belle declared. "Come on, Jim. We're keeping Mr. le Verne from his work."

"You'd best tell Captain Yancy what's happening, Jim," the clerk advised as his visitors turned to depart.

"I'll do just that," Bludso promised.

Leaving the office, Belle and Bludso passed through the hustle and bustle of the Gentlemen's and Ladies' Cabins. Already passengers were coming aboard and being escorted to their accommodations. Stewards and stewardesses were making everything ready for the journey. So there was considerable coming and going on all sides. When the girl and the engineer reached it, the texas deck —on which the officers lived—seemed almost peaceful. The captain, both mates, the pilots and their cubs, and Jim's trio of junior engineers were all attending to their duties. Passengers were discouraged from visiting the texas deck in dock, and none were to be seen.

Belle suggested that it might be tactful if they reported to the captain before Bludso showed her to his quarters. Agreeing that to do so would be sound diplomacy, the engineer said that they would need to go up to the pilot-house.

Towering high in the air, the square, multiwindowed pilothouse was positively tranquil after the hurly-burly of the main and boiler decks. It was one area of a riverboat that had always fascinated Belle—although not one in which she had ever been encouraged to linger when paying a visit. With the great wheel—half of its twelve-foot diameter disappearing into the texas deck below—bells and bell ropes, the whistle's cord, and a speaking tube which connected with the engine room, it was regarded as being male domain.

Belle had liked what she had seen of the tall, lean, smartly dressed Captain Yancy when he had joined them on the dock after the fight. There could not have been a greater contrast than between the master of the *Prairie Belle* and the ruffianly Captain Bascoll. Yancy had been ready to back his engineer to the hilt and had shown that he would stand no nonsense.

Eyeing Belle in a coldly speculative manner, Yancy was nevertheless polite when Bludso introduced her as "Miss Winslow." On being asked for a few words in private, the captain had suggested that they should go along the deck. The pilothouse was occupied. On the long bench at its rear, the pilots were discussing conditions farther down the river with two of their opposite numbers from a boat which had just come up.

"If you wish to do so, I won't raise any objections to your sharing Mr. Bludso's cabin," Yancy declared, after he had heard Belle's reason for making the request and had ascertained that Brunel's presence would not endanger his boat and passengers. "But I'm afraid that I won't be able to offer you a place at my table."

"Of course not," Belle smiled. "People would be suspicious if you did."

While the captain of a riverboat might allow his officers to travel in company with women other than their wives, he could not acknowledge the fact openly. So, although he guessed that Belle was of a social status that might expect the hospitality of his table, he had known that he could not give it.

"One thing more, Miss Winslow," Yancy remarked. "If there should be the slightest hint of danger to the *Belle*—"

"I'll tell you right away," the girl assured him. "But I don't think there will be."

"Neither do I," Yancy said. "If I did, I wouldn't have given you permission to go ahead."

Returning to the texas deck, Bludso opened the door of his cabin and let Belle precede him into it. She looked around at what would be her base of operations for the next few days. There was a homely, yet masculine air about the room. Its furnishings were comfortable and adequate to the needs of a man like Bludso. There was a locker, a washstand, a small writing table and chair, a chest, and a narrow bunk.

"What's that?" Belle inquired, indicating a feminine hat-box in the center of the bunk.

"A hat I've bought for that lil red-headed gal in Helena," Bludso explained, walking forward. "Take a look and tell me if it'll go with her hair."

"How gallant!" Belle sniffed, following on his heels. "Only a bachelor would dare to ask his 'wife's' opinion about a hat he's bought for a lady friend."

Something at the extreme lower edge of the girl's range of vision attracted her attention. It was a small splash of bright color, contrasting vividly with the bare white planks of the deck. While she was speaking, she lowered her gaze to take a closer look. The ends of two blue satin ribbons lay on the floor, extending a little way from beneath the bunk.

"My father 'n' gran'pappy both were lifelong bachelors, and they allus taught me to stay the same," Bludso grinned. Placing the base of the box on the palm of his left hand, he started to lift the lid with his right in a perfect parody of a snooty milliner exposing her latest Parisian creation. "This hat—"

An alarm signal blasted its way through Belle's entire being!

Jumping forward, the girl thrust with the tip of her parasol to knock the box from Bludso's palm. It flew from beneath the lid, landing on the center of the bunk and tipping sideways. Bludso's startled exclamation almost drowned a sudden, sharp, violent hissing which was emanating from inside the box.

Almost, but not quite!

Hearing the sound, Belle and Bludso had a fair notion of what might be making it even before the box discharged its contents. That still did not prevent its appearance from handing them one hell of a surprise and shock.

Something that looked like a four-foot length of rope, as thick as a man's wrist, slid onto the bunk. Except that no piece of rope had ever been plaited with dull brownish, wrinkled skin, sporting an evil spade-shaped head, and endowed with the power to writhe and move under its own volition.

Instead of sliding to the deck, the big Eastern cottonmouth went into its fighting coil on the bed. Vibrating its tail like a rattlesnake, only without the accompanying warning sound, it threw back its head. Opening its mouth to show off the long, curved, poison-dripping fangs and darting, restless forked tongue, it also exposed the snow-white interior which gave the species its name. All in all, it made a frightening sight as it poised ready to attack.

Involuntarily, Belle and Bludso stepped away from the bunk. Their movements brought the furious snake's attention to them. Fortunately, neither was so incapacitated by shock as to be unable to respond.

As swiftly as Bludso sent his right hand flying toward the Ames knife, Belle moved even faster. Her left hand closed on and tugged sharply at the body of the parasol. Separating from the lower half, the handle displayed its clandestine second function.

Swinging her right hand outward horizontally, Belle reversed its direction with a snapping motion of the wrist. Attached to a short steel rod, a small ball of the same metal slid into view. These were followed by a twelve-inch length of powerful coil spring, into which they had been telescoped within the handle. Whipping through the air in an arc, the spring propelled the ball faster than the human eye could follow. Emitting a sickening "thwack!" the ball impacted against the cottonmouth's head. With its deadly skull reduced to a harmless bloody pulp, the snake's body was hurled across the bunk to strike against the cabin's wall.

Shuddering violently, Belle spun on her heel to avoid watching the death throes of the hideous creature. At her side, Bludso was giving off a flow of invective that was violently profane in content, but understandable under the circumstances. He, or Belle, had been very, *very* close to death.

Several seconds went by before either of them regained his, or her, composure. Yet neither spoke until Belle had retrieved and reassembled her parasol and Bludso had returned the knife to its sheath.

"No," Belle finally said, still not looking at the bunk. "I don't think it would go with her hair."

"This one might," Bludso drawled, bending and drawing the hat—the ribbons of which had probably saved his life—from under the bunk. "Only somebody's changed it since I fetched it on board."

"I didn't think you'd done it as a joke," Belle admitted.

"Riled up like it was, that cottonmouth would've killed whoever was nearest to it when it come out of the box," Bludso said quietly. "Thing being, Belle, are they after you or me?"

"You, I'd say," Belle replied. "They couldn't know that I'd be coming here with you, even if they suspected me."

"You're right on that," Bludso growled. "Let me take this blasted thing and heave it into the river. Then we'll go and start asking folks how it got in here."

# 11
## THE COAL TORPEDO!

"I suppose you're happy now you've got the *Stream Queen* behind us," Belle Boyd remarked to Jim Bludso, as they stood at the rear of the engineering section of the *Prairie Belle*'s main deck and looked back along the river.

"Shucks, no," the engineer replied. "It was only a matter of time before we passed her. That hogged-up scow's no match for the *Belle*. She might have pulled out Friday evening, but I knew we'd be leaving her behind before we hit the Baton Royale Glide."

"Do you think that they left the cottonmouth in your cabin, Jim?" Belle inquired, watching the lights and red glow from the *Stream Queen*'s twin, high, flaring-topped, smoke- and sparks-vomiting smokestacks.

"I wouldn't put anything past Bascoll or Tyrone," Bludso growled. "Except that I don't know how they managed to do it, or have it done."

On being informed of the attempted murder, Captain Yancy had insisted that the police be notified. He knew the temper of his engineer and had had no desire for Bludso to commence an independent, unofficial inquiry—especially as the most obvious suspects had appeared to be Bascoll and Tyrone.

Despite all their efforts, the police had not been able to

discover who had placed the snake in Bludso's cabin. On being questioned, Bascoll and Tyrone had presented unshakable alibis. The possibility of their hiring another person to make the attempt had not been overlooked but could not be proven.

There had been a considerable number of people coming and going on the *Prairie Belle* due to the preparations for departure. With so many strangers aboard, none of the crew had noticed any suspicious person or persons lurking around. The simple lock on Bludso's door could have been picked easily, and, with all the officers fully engaged by their various duties, the would-be killer had had ample opportunity to do it. Once in the cabin, he had probably selected the hatbox as the most suitable hiding place for the cottonmouth snake. The Police had concluded that he had hoped Bludso would not open the box until the *Prairie Belle* was on its way downriver.

Although the police had been aware that Bascoll could have organized the attempt, they had known that proving it would be difficult. So, wishing to avert the possibility of open warfare between the two boats, they had allowed the *Stream Queen* to leave at its scheduled time of departure on Friday night.

Much as Belle would have liked to take an active part in the investigation, she had had her own duties to perform. So she had left it in the hands of the police. Returning to the small hotel opposite Molloy's warehouse, she had compared notes with Darren on their activities. She had found that her efforts in securing a berth for him had been needless. Showing more initiative than Belle would have credited him with possessing, Stenhouse had already booked accommodation for all of them. Learning that Stenhouse would be going along had not filled her with delight. However, she could hardly have blamed him for arranging their transportation. Having been uncertain whether Bludso would be aboard the *Prairie Belle,* she had not mentioned her hopes in that direction when discussing plans with Stenhouse.

Working separately, Belle and Darren had continued to keep the consignment under observation. They had never let it out of their sight until it was delivered to the docks and disappeared into the *Prairie Belle*'s hold. While the young man had kept watch to guard against a last-minute change of destination, Belle had collected her belongings from the hotel and transferred them to Bludso's cabin. She had not known whether Stenhouse would approve, but was not worried on that score. Traveling as the engineer's "wife" would allow her greater freedom than if she was occupying the stateroom. With her property aboard, she had relieved Darren so that he could collect his.

That evening, in a carefully arranged, casual-seeming meeting, Darren had given Belle the latest developments. Clearly Stenhouse had been busy, and the results of his enterprise had not been entirely worthless. Calling upon Captain O'Shea in his official capacity, he had obtained information concerning the investigation into the Bijou Theater incident. Apparently the police had given little credence to Belle's anonymous letter, for they had been making no special efforts to locate and arrest Mephisto. They had, however, collected the dead man's property from the Travelers Hotel and contacted the nearest Pinkerton's field office to ask if "Sheriff" had been a member of the National Detective Agency. Belle had been willing to bet that the answer would be negative.

One puzzling factor had emerged from Stenhouse's visit to O'Shea. He had been allowed to examine O'Reilly's effects. The coal torpedoes were no longer in the carpetbag.

That had been a source of some speculation between Belle and Darren. Obviously, O'Reilly's companions had removed the torpedoes rather than allow them to fall into the hands of the police. Also, the organization would not want to lose the weapons if they were to serve as models for future missiles.

Brunel had come on board shortly before the boat's departure. For all the interest he had displayed in the consignment, he might have been nothing more than a professional gambler making a trip. At no time had he gone ashore during the journey. Nor had he displayed more than a casual interest in any other passenger. While he had introduced himself to Darren, using the "mistake" he had made at the hotel as his excuse, he had not attempted to develop a closer acquaintance with the view to obtaining information.

After watching Brunel for a few days, Belle and Darren had come to the conclusion that he was merely supervising the delivery and, in all probability, traveling alone.

Belle had been amused but not perturbed by Stenhouse's reaction to her choice of accommodation. Admitting that her pose of being Bludso's "wife" had its advantages, he had been concerned about her doing so might reflect badly upon the good name of the United States Secret Service. The girl might have explained that his fears were groundless. Although she and Bludso had occupied the cabin every night, nothing sexual was happening outside of Stenhouse's imagination. By a careful arrangement of timing, their undressing and dressing was carried out with as much privacy as possible. While Belle occupied the bunk, Bludso had bedded down on the floor.

Once satisfied that Brunel did not suspect her, Belle had reverted to wearing the Hessian boots and riding breeches under her skirt and had donned a somewhat more decorous blouse.

The journey had been uneventful and pleasant. As Jim Bludso's "wife," Belle could come and go as she pleased with one exception. Her presence in the Ladies' Cabin had not been encouraged. That did not worry her, for she was accepted in the gentlemen's section of the boiler deck's huge, stateroom-lined saloon, and her visits to the main deck had aroused no comment.

To help pass the time, Belle had fallen into the habit of

joining Bludso on the main deck every evening. There she had seen much of interest which she had previously taken for granted. She had also become aware of why a riverboat's engineer was regarded as being as important to the vessel's well-being as the captain or the pilot.

Not only did Bludso have to supervise the ceaseless work of his Negro stokers, who were commanded by Willie, but he was also responsible for manipulating the controls. Responding to instructions via the pilothouse's voice pipe, he kept the two enormous side-wheels turning at the required speeds for propelling or maneuvering the *Prairie Belle*'s vast bulk.

From Bludso and Willie, Belle had learned the simple code by which the riverboat engineers lived. Always tend to and care for the engines; heed the pilot's bell and instructions; never let the boat be passed by another.

Attempting to uphold the last condition had been the cause of many a disaster. Boilers had exploded because they had been subjected to excessive pressures and strains. In the excitement of the races, boats had been run aground or had struck snags—fallen trees carried by the current until sinking one end into the river's bed—although that had been the pilots' fault rather than the engineers'.

Even without racing, the danger of fire was always very real upon the riverboats. Due to the vessel's specialized requirements, it had to have its superstructure constructed as lightly as possible. In addition to making use of the thinnest available timbers, every top-class boat had to be well painted and carry much decorative carving and fretwork which rendered it highly inflammable.

To further save weight, the boats were powered by engines working at high pressures of at least 120 pounds per square inch—using standard types of locomotive boilers fed by a general service pump known as the "doctor." The small, rapidly steaming boilers—each vessel carried sufficient to power the paddle wheels—were wood burners and required a large grate area to ensure complete combus-

tion. This could not be obtained, so the chimney stacks
vomited out sparks, flames, and glowing embers among the
clouds of black smoke. The sun-dried nature of the vessel's
timbers needed little encouragement to catch fire.

"We ain't never had a fire on the *Belle*," Willie had told
the girl on the night before they had reached her old
hometown of Baton Royale. "And I sure enough hopes we
never does."

"I should think so," Belle had replied. "It would be terrible."

"Massa Jim always allows that if it happens, he'll hold
her nozzle again' the bank while everybody gets ashore,"
Willie went on.

"He's just about cussed enough to do it," Belle had
praised, visualizing what would happen to Bludso if he
should ever be compelled to keep his promise.

On arriving in Baton Royale, Belle had found the *Stream
Queen* at the landing stage. Despite having reached the
town ahead of the *Prairie Belle*, the other boat had not
taken its departure when the *Belle* had cast off.

There had been considerable delight among the crew of
the *Prairie Belle* at finding themselves ahead of their hated
rivals. When Belle had inquired about the reason for the
*Stream Queen*'s delay, she had been treated to a variety of
possible motives. One had been that Bascoll did not dare
take his ramshackle old bucket through the Baton Royale
Glide after nightfall.

Of all the reasons, that had been the one which struck
Belle as the least likely. A mile below Baton Royale, some
freak of the terrain caused the river to flow fast and deep
with hardly any shallows. On either side, the shoreline fell
away steeply from the man-made levee bank into at least
ten feet of water. Although the current would thrust a boat
along at a fair speed, the area was not regarded as being
particularly dangerous. So she had concluded that the
crew's summation was founded more on contempt for Bascoll's abilities than upon actual fact.

"Did it hurt you, seeing Baton Royale again?" Bludso inquired, turning his back on the *Stream Queen*.

"A little," Belle admitted. "But I couldn't see where my home used to be from the landing, and I didn't want to go ashore in case somebody recognized me."

"Is that why you've stayed on board at all the other halts?" Bludso asked with a grin.

"*You* know it's not," Belle replied. "If I'd landed, I'd probably have wound up fighting off one of my many rivals."

"Shucks, there ain't that many of them," Bludso protested. "It just seems that way."

"I'm sure it does," Belle said, smiling. "Did your red-haired friend like her hat?"

"She sure did," Bludso confirmed. Then his face lost its smile. "Damn it, Belle, it *had* to be Bascoll— But I don't see how they managed to set it up in time."

"Or me," Belle said soberly. "Have you any other enemies?"

"None'd go that far," Bludso replied.

Motives for the attempted killing had been discussed many times during the journey but were doomed to be forgotten that night. Underfoot, Belle could sense that a force almost as powerful as the *Prairie Belle*'s paddle wheels was gripping the hull and carrying them forward. Even more aware of the change, Bludso walked in the direction of the controls. Until they had passed through the Glide, he would be constantly on the alert for the pilot's instructions.

Walking at Bludso's side, Belle looked along the lamp-lit deck. Negro stokers were feeding cordwood into the yawning, glowing mouths of the furnaces, but they did not hold her attention. Up by the forward boiler, Willie was speaking to the gambler, Brunel. Even as Belle watched, the white man swung away from the Negro and walked—hurried would have been a better word—toward the stairs leading to the boiler deck.

"What did Brunel want down here?" the girl asked.

"That's what I'm wondering," Bludso replied. Then, as Willie came up ready to support him in the passage through the Glide, he repeated Belle's question.

"Allowed he'd spilled ink all over his carpetbag and spoiled most of his clothes," the Negro answered. "So he'd bundled 'em up and fetched 'em down to get shut of 'em. I was too late to stop him pitching them in."

"The coal torpedoes!" Belle shrieked.

All in a single flash of intuition, the girl had seen the answers to many of her assignment's puzzling questions.

At last she knew why O'Reilly had spoken the truth to Darren about the consignment's departure. She also understood why he had been carrying the coal torpedoes in his carpetbag and why the organization had taken the chance of robbing the hotel to retrieve them. Brunel's lack of activity had also been explained. So had the references made by Andy and Mick outside the warehouse with regard to *finishing* the trip on Bascoll's boat.

Everything was suddenly, frighteningly, almost unbelievably clear!

Regrettably, Belle's understanding had come just too late!

With a thunderous roar and a sheet of raging flame, the forward boiler exploded. Blazing chunks of wood flew in all directions. The furnace's stoker screamed briefly but hideously as the sheet of leaping fire engulfed him. Such was the force of the detonation that the *Prairie Belle*'s massive bulk heaved ponderously. Its starboard paddle wheel lifted clear of the water, spinning wildly and hurling spray; then it regained an even keel.

Thrown off balance, Belle was flung against the control panel. Bludso's weight collided with her and sandwiched her against the board. Winded and unconscious, she slid to the deck as he lurched away. The incident had one benefit. Cushioned by Belle's slender body, Bludso suffered no injury and retained the use of his faculties.

With the effects of the explosion felt throughout the boat, pandemonium reigned. Seeing the fire growing rapidly, the deck passengers, roustabouts, and stokers who had not been flung overboard hurled themselves into the river. Their actions were understandable, for they could see the full threat of the conflagration.

On the boiler deck, glassware and crockery cascaded to ruins on the floor. Men and women went sprawling in all directions. Screams, shouts, crashes, and moans filled the air. Lamps left their hangers and rained down to create further fires.

Clinging to the handgrips of the wheel, the pilot had managed to avoid deserting his post. Ignoring his visitors, who had been tumbled from the bench at the rear of the pilothouse, he followed the instructions laid down by Captain Yancy for such an emergency. Without needing to check, he knew which was the nearer bank. So, catching his balance, he swung hard on the wheel. Heeling slightly as the push of the current caught her, the *Prairie Belle* responded to the helm and started to turn. The pilot hoped that Jim Bludso was at the engine's controls. Without him, the boat would not be able to fight the pressure of the river and complete its turn toward the shore.

On the main deck, Bludso shook his head and sprang to the controls. Like the pilot, he had learned the proposed drill to be followed in the event of a fire. No instructions had come from the pilothouse, but the engineer knew what he must do. Being closest to the port bank, they would head in that direction. So Bludso reduced the revolutions of the left side-wheel. He knew that merely directing the bows against the levee would not be sufficient. The boat would have to be held in position for long enough to present the passengers with an opportunity of escaping. So the wheels must be kept turning—and that could only be done from the engineer's control panel.

Bludso knew just how slight his chances of getting clear

in time would be, but he did not let that lessen his resolve to continue doing his duty.

"Willie!" the engineer called, trying to see through the flames. "Are you all right?"

"Shook is all," answered the Negro. "What can I do for you?"

"Get Belle ashore."

"I can't leave you, Massa Jim!"

"You can. There's no sense in us both staying. And I want to know that somebody'll be around to tell the truth about the explosion."

"But—" Willie groaned.

"Do like I tell you!" Bludso roared. "You've never failed me afore, old friend."

"I'll do like you says," Willie promised, bending to lift the unconscious girl from the deck.

"Another thing," Bludso put in. "Before you go, take my old Ames knife—and when you lay hands on that bastard Brunel, use it for me."

# 12
# THERE'S NO WAY YOU CAN STOP ME

"Brunel escaped from the *Prairie Belle*," Belle Boyd told General Handiman as they sat in Stenhouse's hotel suite at New Orleans. "Darren saw him on shore, but we lost contact with him after that."

"He wasn't aboard the *Stream Queen* when she arrived," the head of the Secret Service replied. "I had Lieutenant St. Andre of the New Orleans Police Department* make a search as soon as it docked."

Belle was once more the elegant, fashionable lady, dressed in an outfit which she had purchased in Baton Royale. Yet her face showed signs of grief and of the deep strain she had been under. She had had little rest since the night of the *Prairie Belle*'s fire.

Carried onto the levee by Willie, the girl had recovered consciousness in time to see the end of the drama.

Due to Jim Bludso's gallant act of self-sacrifice, the blazing boat's bow had been held against the river's bank while all its other occupants had fled. The engineer had stuck to his post until the end, going through what must have been hell as the flames raged higher and the heat became unendurable in its intensity. Boiler after boiler had exploded,

* *Details of Lieutenant St. Andre's career are given in* The Bullwhip Breed.

ripping the once-magnificent vessel to pieces. Knowing that he had no hope of surviving, Jim Bludso had carried out his promise at the cost of his own life.

Learning what had happened from Willie, Belle had immediately started to search for Brunel. Darren had seen the gambler on the levee, but they could find no trace of him there or in the town of Baton Royale. Remembering Andy's comment about having to finish the ride to New Orleans on Bascoll's boat, Belle had insisted that Stenhouse telegraph to Madame Lucienne and ask for her to arrange to have the gambler arrested when the *Stream Queen* arrived. Carrying out Belle's instructions, Stenhouse had also asked that accommodation be arranged for himself and his two agents.

Taking the first available boat, Belle, Willie, Darren, and Stenhouse had journeyed down to New Orleans. They had been met at the dock by Madame Lucienne's Negro maid bringing a letter from her employer. In it had been instructions as to the hotel at which she had arranged for the two men and Belle to stay. To Belle's delight, Lucienne had also sent along her trunk. Learning where he could contact Belle, Willie had set off alone in search of the man who had been responsible for his friend's death. Before they had separated, Belle had obtained the Negro's promise that he would inform her as soon as he had located Brunel. She had also asked that, if possible, Brunel should not be harmed before she was on hand. It was her intention to try to take the man alive and induce him to answer her questions.

On the point of going to visit Madame Lucienne as a start in her hunt for Brunel, Belle had been summoned to Stenhouse's suite. Darren, who had delivered the message, had agreed to go to Lucienne's fashionable and exclusive dress shop immediately. There he would tell the woman everything that had happened and save any further waste of time. Much to her surprise, Belle had found that General Handiman was with the coordinator.

While going through her story for Handiman's benefit, Belle had seen him show a hint of puzzlement on more than one occasion—particularly when she mentioned a point that had not struck her as being consistent with the other facts. At the same time, Stenhouse had displayed a growing alarm and apprehension.

"Anyway," Stenhouse remarked, exhibiting an air of relief which did not ring true, "at least the consignment will never reach Ireland."

"I wouldn't be too sure of that," Belle replied.

Big, heavily built, Handiman looked more like a prosperous businessman or planter than the head of the United States Secret Service. He glanced at Belle in a speculative manner as she spoke.

"Why is that, Miss Boyd?" he asked.

"There's no way they could recover the rifles," Stenhouse went on. "Even assuming that any could have survived the explosions. The river—"

"I know all that!" Belle interrupted. "And I'm sure the Irishmen planned everything so we'd be led to such a conclusion."

"Go on, please," Handiman requested, waving Stenhouse to remain silent.

"It all fits," Belle obliged. "They knew that we were on to their game and wanted to throw us off the track. So, somewhere or other, they transferred the rifles and ammunition to other containers. Then they let the bales and weighted boxes go on the *Prairie Belle,* making sure that Darren knew about it. O'Reilly, or whatever his name was, should have accompanied the shipment. When he was killed, Brunel took his place. They planned to wreck the boat in an area where, even if we wanted to check, it would be impossible to do so. The Baton Royale Glide was the finest place for their purpose."

"The uniforms, boots, and hats were on the boat," Stenhouse reminded her.

"What use would the Irish nationalists have for them?"

Belle answered. "The rifles would be useful, but they wouldn't need uniforms. And leaving the bales intact, making sure that Darren could see and identify the contents, did much to divert attention from the possibility of the boxes not containing rifles and ammunition."

"They've gone to a lot of trouble just for a hundred rifles," Handiman remarked. "Of course, that many repeaters might go a long way in winning Ireland back for the Pope."

"How's that?" Belle inquired, a vague recollection of something she had been told struggling to burst through her memory.

"Didn't you know?" Handiman said, smiling. "I'm assured, by an Irish waiter in my Washington club, that is what they're trying to do."

"Then it's not likely that an Irish Protestant would be helping them?"

"I'd say it's highly *unlikely,* Miss Boyd," Handiman corrected. "Why do you ask?"

"Because Darren said that O'Reilly had agreed to work for him out of dislike for Molloy," Belle answered.

"And—" Handiman prompted.

"According to O'Reilly, Molloy was a 'Protestant son of a bitch,'" the girl elaborated. "He is also one of the few Irishmen involved in the affair. 'O'Reilly' and Opal certainly weren't. Nor were Brunel and Bascoll. And I heard mention of somebody they called 'the Frenchman' as one of the leaders."

"The two men who made the purchase were French—" Stenhouse began.

"Who spoke with such obvious Irish accents that they aroused suspicion," Belle put in. "I've little respect for nationalist agitators of any kind, but I don't believe they would be *that* stupid."

"You think that somebody other than Irish nationalists might be involved, Miss Boyd?" Handiman inquired, darting a cold glare at the coordinator who was showing increasing alarm.

"It's possible, though I can't think who," the girl replied. "Everything points to them being Irish. Perhaps too obviously. Men with French names and Irish accents would be sure to start us thinking on the required lines. Using Molloy's—an Irishman's—warehouse kept us thinking that way. So did 'O'Reilly's' adopting a brogue when he was dealing with Darren. And giving a typical Irishman's excuse, religious bigotry, for betraying his employer. Even the name they had given to the consignors of the shipment, the 'Shamrock Supplies Incorporated,' would help keep us thinking they were Irish."

"I'm inclined to agree with you," Handiman declared.

"Thank you," Belle answered. "Perhaps you can tell me who, other than the Irish, they might be."

"You mean that you haven't told her?" Handiman growled, staring at his worried-looking male subordinate.

"Well, sir," Stenhouse began hesitantly. "You see— That is—"

"What haven't I been told?" Belle demanded suspiciously.

"There are men in the South fomenting discontent and advocating that the Southern States should secede from the Union," Handiman elaborated. "According to our reports, they are hoping to stir up an armed rebellion."

"The Ku Klux Klan?" Belle asked.

"They've practically disbanded now that the worst excesses of Reconstruction have been ended," Handiman replied. "It's possible that some of the Klan's more radical members are involved, but we've no proof of that. In fact, we've no concrete evidence of their existence, other than fairly reliable rumors."

"And did Mr. Stenhouse know of these rumors?" Belle said icily.

"Well—er—yes," Stenhouse spluttered. "I had heard of them."

"Then why didn't you mention them to me?" the girl blazed. "If I'd known, it might have opened up a whole new line of thought."

"I didn't think that it had any connection—" Stenhouse commenced.

"The hell you didn't!" Belle shouted, springing from her chair with such velocity that it went flying backward across the room. "You didn't *trust* me enough to mention it, if it might involve Southrons. I'm the Rebel Spy."

"That's nothing to do with—" Stenhouse yelped, also rising and registering alarm before the girl's barely controlled fury.

"You're a rotten, stinking liar, Stenhouse!" Belle yelled, tensing as if to fling herself in a savage attack at the cringing, pallid man. "You didn't mind General Handiman bringing me into it to cover your nephew's inadequacies, as long as only Irish nationalists were involved—"

"Really, General Handiman!" Stenhouse spluttered. "This is intolerable—"

"What happened to Jim Bludso and the *Prairie Belle* was intolerable too!" the girl thundered, making an almost visible mental effort to restrain herself from taking violent physical action.

"That's enough, both of you!" Handiman barked, slapping a big hand hard on the top of the table. "Bickering between ourselves—"

*"Bickering!"* Belle spat out the word viciously. "God! If I'd only known—"

"You'd have seen everything in a flash, *Colonel* Boyd?" Handiman challenged, for the first time using the rank which Belle had been given to enhance her official standing and to help when dealing with military or civil authorities.

"Perhaps not," the girl admitted. "But I might have suspected—"

"There are *some* who might say that you ought to have suspected what was going to happen as soon as you heard that the coal torpedoes had been stolen from 'O'Reilly's' carpetbag," Handiman pointed out, glaring the other man into silence and anticipating his comment. "It's all too easy to say what one should, or could, or ought to have done, after the event."

"It is," Belle conceded, "but, if I *had* been told—"

*"Perhaps* things would have been different," Handiman finished for her. "Nobody could have conceived that they would take such an extreme step, endangering hundreds of lives, to destroy a fake cargo and throw us off their trail."

"I believe that they were counting on a large loss of life, so that we wouldn't believe they would have done such a thing," Belle said bitterly. "That's why they had the snake left in Jim Bludso's cabin. They'd heard of his claim that, if the *Prairie Belle* caught fire, he would hold the bows against the bank until everybody got ashore. That wouldn't have suited their ends. So they wanted him out of the way."

"Which you can see now, *after* the event," Handiman pointed out gently. "Our present concern is not to lay the blame, but to decide on what action we must take against these people."

"I'm going after whoever's responsible," Belle declared.

"Even if they are Southrons?" asked the coordinator, stung into indiscretion by the challenging glare which the girl had directed his way.

*"Mister!"* Belle hissed. "I swore the oath of allegiance to the Union before I joined the Secret Service. Since then *I've* been in the field, carrying out dangerous assignments, not sitting behind a desk coordinating. There has never been any question against my loyalty. If that doesn't satisfy you, I'll resign right now."

"It satisfies *me*," Handiman stated, and gave added strength to the words by crossing the room to collect the girl's chair.

"Apart from realizing that no good could come from

another attempt at secession," Belle went on, sitting down, "I've personal reasons for getting them, whoever they are."

"Personal reasons?" queried Handiman.

"When I went to Jim Bludso for help, he agreed to give it without even asking what I wanted. Despite the fact that he suspected what I was doing and how helping me could be dangerous. Helping me caused his death. That's all the reason I need for avenging him. There's no way you can stop me going after them."

"You can't conduct a private vendetta, no matter what was between you—" Stenhouse put in.

"Don't you even finish *that!*" Belle warned the coordinator. "Even if Jim and I *had* bedded down together every night, it wouldn't have been any of your damned concern. But we didn't, although we slept in the same cabin. To satisfy your filthy little mind, Jim slept on the floor."

"I—I—" Stenhouse spluttered.

"There's no need for you to go on, Colonel Boyd," Handiman announced, cutting off the other man's protests. "Your morals are not being questioned and neither is your loyalty."

"Do you concur, Mr. Coordinator?" Belle challenged.

"I agree with General Handiman," Stenhouse confirmed with humility. "Although I want to go on record as saying that you misinterpreted the comment I was going to make. I apologize, ma'am."

"Then I accept your apology, sir," Belle replied. "What do we know about these Southron agitators?"

"Very little, beyond the fact that they do exist and have been very busy," Handiman replied. "Nothing important or too dangerous, but active. So far, they have restricted their efforts to making inflammatory speeches or appeals for funds—"

"The fund-raising was one of the reasons I didn't take them more seriously," Stenhouse announced in hopeful self-exculpation. "I believed that they were no more than a bunch of confidence tricksters duping the unwary."

"And as long as they were only doing it to Southrons, that was all right," Belle drawled sardonically.

"No!" Stenhouse yelped. "Of course not. It just didn't seem to come under our jurisdiction.

"Madame Lucienne thought that it could become serious," Handiman injected, directing a cold glare of remonstration at Belle. "That's why I'm down here. As soon as I saw in which direction the consignment was heading. I wondered if we might have been deliberately misled by the purchasers."

"One hundred repeating rifles wouldn't be a big factor in helping the South to secede," Belle remarked. "But it would be a start. It might even appeal to the agitators' sense of humor to know that the first weapons of the new conflict had been purchased from a regiment that had been organized to fight us."

"That's part of it," Handiman guessed. "Mainly, though, the purchase of so many arms would arouse interest. So they selected a way that would mislead us if news of it should leak out."

"What do we do now?" Stenhouse inquired.

"Any ideas on *that*, Colonel Boyd?" Handiman requested.

"Not until I've seen Lucienne," the girl admitted. Then a thought struck her. "Where is the *Stream Queen* now?"

"She went north again on the morning after she arrived," Handiman replied. "There was no legal reason for holding her. I had her stopped and searched before she reached Baton Rouge. Brunel wasn't on board."

"Then he must be in the city," Belle breathed.

"That's likely," Handiman agreed. "We can't cover every exit, but we're watching those he's most likely to use if he wants to leave. And we've men alerted to watch for him all through Louisiana."

Belle was less impressed by the information than Stenhouse seemed to be. There were too many ways by which Brunel could have escaped from New Orleans. Nor would the watchers, armed with no more than descriptions, be guaranteed to identify him. In a few days, they could be supplied with copies of Darren's excellent sketch, but by that time it might be too late.

"Lord!" the girl said fervently. "Let him still be in New Orleans. If he is, Willie might find him."

*"Willie?"* Handiman questioned.

"Jim Bludso's Negro stoker," the girl elaborated. "If there's nothing more, General, I'll be going."

"What if you can't find Brunel?" Stenhouse asked as she stood up.

"One of the men at the warehouse said that something was going to happen in Shreveport," Belle replied. "If I don't find him, I'll go and make another start from there."

"This time you can count on *every* cooperation," Handiman assured her.

"Thank you for *that,"* Belle answered and walked out of the room.

Leaving the suite, Belle went out of the hotel and found a cab. While riding to Madame Lucienne's establishment, she started to think about the latest developments.

If she had only known about the Southron agitators!

That damned fool Stenhouse and his mistrust . . .

Yet there had been cause—if unjust and unfounded—for it. During the War, Belle had been a very successful spy and had given loyal, devoted service to the Confederate cause. She could hardly blame a man like the coordinator for being wary where Southron interests were concerned. In his place, she might have experienced similar misgivings.

For all that, if Stenhouse had been frank with her, she might have connected the coal torpedoes with the shipment and the *Prairie Belle.* She had been aware of the possibility that they were on a wild-goose chase. Possibly she would have anticipated a means by which the Secret Service could be thrown completely off the trail. The purpose of coal torpedoes was primarily to blow up and destroy ships. They would have an extremely limited use in the

"liberation" of Ireland. And, more to the point, they offered a solution that would be only too obvious to a Southron mind.

Of course, as General Handiman had said, it was hell-
ishly easy to be wise *after* the event.

Who could have foreseen how the agitators would be so
disdainful of human lives that they would deliberately
wreck the riverboat?

Forcing herself to become calm, for she found her body
shaking and trembling with the fury of her emotions, Belle
settled more firmly on the seat. She accepted that she
would gain nothing by mulling feverishly over the past.
That could not be changed, whether it had been right or
wrong. What mattered was the future. So she gave her
thoughts to what lay ahead.

Nothing that Belle might have imagined could have
equalled the shock of the next development.

Leaving and paying off the cab, the girl looked at the
darkened display windows of Lucienne's shop. The drapes
had been drawn at the windows of the living quarters, but a
glimmer of lamplight showed through. So Belle went to the
right-hand alley, knowing that there was a side entrance
which she could use. Turning the corner, she came face to
face with Darren.

Such was the shock and horror on the young man's face
that Belle slammed to a halt and felt a terrible sensation of
foreboding. He hardly seemed to recognize her as she
blocked his path.

"What is it?" Belle gasped.

"Must . . . get . . . doctor!" Darren croaked.

At that moment Belle became aware that the side door
was open.

"Lucienne!" she exclaimed.

"D-don't go up!" the man warned, catching her left
bicep as she started to brush by him.

Wrenching her arm free, Belle ran along the alley and
entered the building. The Negro maid sprawled in the hall,

dead, with her throat cut from ear to ear. Sobbing in anxiety, Belle raced up the stairs. Although she had known that something must be terribly wrong, she was unprepared for exactly what met her gaze.

Completely naked, her arms and ankles lashed to the posts, Lucienne was spread-eagled upon the bed. Her plump body bore numerous horrible abrasions, as if whole chunks of flesh had been plucked from it. A further horror was that each nipple had been ripped from its breast. There was a gag in her mouth. Despite the bloody stab wound in her stomach, the movement of the bosom and feeble struggles showed that she was alive.

Slowly Lucienne's head turned toward the door. Her eyes opened. Showing the torments she must be suffering, they held recognition too. Flinging herself across the room, Belle jerked free the gag with shaking hands.

"Who did it?" the girl demanded.

"Paul de Bracy," Lucienne moaned, slurring her words yet making them audible. "One de Bracy called 'the Frenchman'—and Alvin Brunel."

# 13
# YOU'LL NEVER MAKE
# ME TALK

Swinging his silver-capped walking stick jauntily, Paul de Bracy strolled from the house in which he was supposed to have remained hidden until arrangements could be made for him to join Alvin Brunel and leave New Orleans. The time was ten o'clock on the evening after he had helped to deal with the traitress Madame Lucienne. Against his orders, and in the face of common sense, he was going to visit a lady of his acquaintance.

Tall, slim, very handsome, every inch the proud, haughty Creole dandy, de Bracy was a recent enlistee in the ranks of the Brotherhood for Southron Freedom. However, he believed that his social standing—reduced as it might have been by the War—automatically rated him worthy of a high place in the organization. That was, indirectly, why he was acting in such a reckless manner.

If only the Frenchman—how he hated that name—had not been so all-fired uppity and had phrased his words as helpful advice to a social equal instead of snapping them out like orders, de Bracy would have been more inclined to comply. In which case, he would have ignored the message, delivered by a tall, burly Negro, inviting him to go to Marie Larondel's apartment and resume their intermittent yet enjoyable amatory association.

Fancying himself as a veritable lady-killer and God's answer to every woman's dreams, de Bracy had not paused to ponder on the means by which Marie had learned of his present whereabouts. He had been brooding too heavily upon the Frenchman's assumption of superiority and had seen Marie's offer only as a way to regain his injured self-respect. Not only was her apartment more to his taste than his present accommodation in a small, middle-rent district house, but by going there he would assert his independence and demonstrate a complete rejection of the Frenchman's self-appointed authority.

Not only had de Bracy objected to being given orders, but he felt that the Frenchman's summation of the situation was wrong. Certainly, from what de Bracy could gather, things had not gone entirely to plan higher up the Mississippi River. However, he believed that the main object of the exercise had been achieved. The fake cargo had been destroyed, as planned, and—he felt sure—its going would have thrown the Secret Service off the genuine shipment's trail. Only the—to de Bracy—unimportant side elements had misfired.

The cottonmouth snake which Brunel had contrived to conceal in Jim Bludso's cabin had failed to do its work. So had an attempt by Bascoll and Tyrone to cripple him in a fight. In de Bracy's opinion, there had been too much emphasis placed on removing the engineer of the *Prairie Belle*. Apparently the Frenchman and other senior members of the Brotherhood had been impressed by Bludso's often-repeated vow that, in case of fire, he would stay at his post and hold the boat against the shore so that the passengers could escape. They had said that if he should succeed in doing this, there was a chance that an investigation of the remains would reveal that the arms and ammunition had not been on board. De Bracy considered that their selection of a point for the wrecking, along the Baton Royale Glide, would have rendered such an investigation impossible even if the boat went down by the bank. He did not know it, but there had been another reason for the attempted assassination.*

In one way, Bludso's staying alive had probably rendered Brunel's work less risky. Instead of having to leap into the water and swim for the shore, he had been able to land dryshod and get aboard the *Stream Queen*, which had halted at the foot of the Glide to collect him and such other passengers who had been willing to purchase a passage to New Orleans.

Fortunately, as it had proved, Brunel had kept his wits about him. The Secret Service agent, Darren, had seen him on the levee. More than that, Darren had apparently connected him with the destruction of the boat and telegraphed to New Orleans to arrange for him to be arrested. Alert for the possibility, Brunel had left the boat five miles clear of New Orleans. He had sent a message to the Frenchman, by Bascoll, and de Bracy had been assigned the task of collecting him.

During the ride to town, Brunel had bitterly cursed himself for not having followed the line of action planned by "O'Reilly": keeping out of Darren's sight on the *Prairie Belle*, then killing and dumping the agent overboard at the first opportunity. By failing to do so, Brunel had been compelled to remain in New Orleans while the Frenchman had set off to take part in some enterprise at Shreveport. Much as de Bracy would have liked to go along, the Frenchman had imperiously ordered him to stay in New Orleans.

Not that de Bracy had regretted the separation from the Frenchman. There was something cold-blooded and sadis-

---

* *In view of his work with the Confederate States Secret Service during the War, Bludso had been invited to attend a meeting and join the Brotherhood. He had declined to enlist but had sworn an oath that he would never reveal the existence of the organization. The Frenchman had insisted that they could not rely upon Bludso's remaining silent, so he must be eliminated.*

*That Bludso meant to keep his word is certain. Although he had guessed Belle's mission concerned the Brotherhood, he had not spoken of it. If Belle had been aware of the facts, she would have understood the correct meaning of Bascoll's calling Bludso a traitor.*

tic about him which repelled the young Creole. De Bracy
thought that he was tough, but he had been almost sick-
ened by the way in which the Frenchman had treated Madame Lucienne. Not that he had opposed her being killed,
for she had come too close to the Brotherhood for comfort
or safety.

According to the Frenchman, somebody had been informing on their activities to Madame Lucienne and she
was now a member of the Yankee Secret Service. So he, de
Bracy, and Brunel had set off to discover the identity of the
informer and to silence the woman.

Arriving at the shop just as Madame Lucienne had been
about to close, they had overpowered her. Knocking her
out, they had locked the front door and taken her upstairs.
Under the Frenchman's guidance, they had stripped her
and lashed her to the bed. They had just brought her back
to consciousness when there had been a sound downstairs.
While the Frenchman had gone to investigate, de Bracy—
whom Lucienne had recognized—had given her a warning
of her danger. He had not used the Frenchman's real
name, but she had clearly recognized his pseudonym. For
all that, and despite being told that the Frenchman had slit
her maid's throat, she had refused to answer their questions.

Gagged, so that she could not scream, Lucienne had
been put through purgatory as the Frenchman clutched,
twisted, and tore at her flesh with the jaws of a powerful
pair of pincers he had brought along. Give the old woman
her due, she had taken everything the Frenchman had
done without yielding. Goaded to fury by his failure, he
had finally hurled the pincers down and, drawing a knife,
stabbed her in the stomach. Nor would he allow Brunel to
finish her off, insisting that they should allow her to die in
agony. Knowing the Frenchman's temper when crossed or
opposed in his desires, Brunel and de Bracy had acceded
to his demands. Letting themselves out of and locking the
front door, they had departed in the belief that Lucienne

would be dead long before anybody missed her and investigated.

Apparently that hope had been justified. The local newspapers had not announced that the two murders had been discovered. Nor had there been any mention of Brunel's part in the destruction of the *Prairie Belle,* which appeared to be dismissed as another riverboat disaster. So de Bracy was under the opinion that the Frenchman had been alarmed for nothing. Or perhaps he was motivated by a desire to lessen the share of the honors and acclaim to be gained in the success of whatever was planned in Shreveport.

De Bracy's train of thought was interrupted by the sight of a carriage halted at the edge of the sidewalk. Turning from where she had been crouching over a huddled shape seated against the front wheel, a slender, shapely, fashionably dressed young woman approached him. In a rougher part of the city, on such a deserted street, de Bracy might have been more alert and cautious. However, the woman's appearance and the respectable aspect of the neighborhood lulled him into a sense of false security.

"Can I help you, ma'am?" de Bracy inquired, doffing his hat.

"Why I just hope you can, sir," the woman replied, her voice cultured and well educated. "My coachman has fallen asleep, and I do believe he's been drinking. Could you help me rouse him?"

"I think I can," de Bracy confirmed and went to kick the seated figure with his toe. "Wake up, damn—"

The Creole had not replaced his hat, which proved to have been a regrettable oversight on his part. Belle Boyd produced a short rubber billy from her vanity bag, took aim, and swung it. Caught at the base of the skull, de Bracy's knees buckled, and he sprawled unconscious across Darren's legs.

"I hope this is him, Belle," Darren remarked, rolling the limp body from his legs and rising to his feet.

"It is," the girl replied. "Willie knows him from delivering the message and signaled when he came out. Here's Willie now. Let's get de Bracy into the carriage. This isn't the best neighborhood in which to carry out a kidnaping."

Having left Belle to do what she could for the stricken dying woman, Darren had gone to fetch a doctor and the police. Lucienne had known that she had no hope of remaining alive, so she had been determined to help Belle locate her attackers. Showing how every word was taking an effort of will and causing her untold agony, she had told the girl where she had concealed her reports on the Brotherhood for Southron Freedom. She had, however, lapsed into unconsciousness before she could describe her assailants.

Without waiting for Darren to return, Belle had removed the knob from the left upper bedpost and extracted the papers it held. With Lucienne on her way to a hospital, although the doctor had stated there was no hope of saving her life, the agents had left the police in charge of the shop. Leaving Darren to return and report to General Handiman, Belle had followed the ambulance. While waiting in the hope that her friend might recover and give more details, Belle had read the reports.

There had been little new added to the girl's sum of knowledge. Lucienne had listed the names of several members, but warned that—to the best of her knowledge—they were not the leaders of the Brotherhood. There was a comment on the organization's activities and a note that there would be a meeting of a different, more significant nature, held in Shreveport. Wise in her work, Lucienne had been alert to the possibility of the reports falling into the wrong hands. So she had avoided leaving any clue to the identity of her informer. Belle had guessed that the name would have been passed on to her orally when she and Lucienne had come together.

Lucienne had died without recovering consciousness. However, Lieutenant St. Andre—who had been assigned

to the case—had promised every cooperation in locating
the men responsible for her death. He had also promised
to keep the story out of the newspapers and had succeeded
in doing so. However, he had pointed out the difficulties in
finding the three men. To the best of his knowledge, none
of them had criminal records. That would make his work
doubly difficult. He had known de Bracy, but not inti-
mately. Using the Creole as a starting point, St. Andre had
commenced his investigations. He would, he had warned,
be working under the handicap of the necessity to prevent
any warning of his Department's interest being passed to
de Bracy.

Appreciating the difficulties faced by the police, Belle
had been relieved to find another means of locating de
Bracy.

In some way, which he described scantily as "having got
the word," Willie had learned of Lucienne's death and
where to find Belle. Already he had started a widespread
and capable net moving in search of Brunel, but without
results. Given another name to work on, he had promised
to do what he could.

Being employed in various capacities at all levels of soci-
ety, Negroes were almost ubiquitous in New Orleans. They
became party to their employers' affairs and frequently
were in possession of what should have been stoutly and
strictly kept secrets. What one Negro knew, he would usually pass on to another.

By eight o'clock on the evening after Lucienne's death,
Willie had not only known where de Bracy was in hiding,
but had learned a number of personal and confidential
details about his private life. On hearing about his association with an actress, Marie Larondel, Belle had selected a
means by which they might induce him to leave the house
and fall into their hands. She wished to capture him without his host—who was on Lucienne's list of the Brotherhood—being aware of his predicament. So she, Willie, and
Darren had made their arrangements. The Negro had de-

livered the fake message, not only to lure de Bracy out but
to make certain they collected the right man.

Lifting the unconscious Creole between them, Willie
and Darren thrust him aboard the carriage. Then the Negro clambered onto the box while Belle and Darren
climbed inside. To make sure that de Bracy did not recover
and create a disturbance, Belle had brought along a bottle
of chloroform. By using it when he showed signs of returning to consciousness, she kept him silent during the
journey to the place she had selected for his interrogation.

Aided by cold water dashed into his face and the acrid,
biting fumes of the smelling salts which Belle held under
his nose, de Bracy recovered from the effects of the blow
and the chloroform. Moaning, he tried to sit up. Finding
himself unable to do so, he twisted and tugged at the ropes
which bound his wrists and ankles.

Conscious thought returned through his throbbing head
and despite the nausea caused by the chloroform. He realized that he was lying on a bed and bound, with a gag in his
mouth, in the same way they had treated Madame
Lucienne.

*Exactly* in the same way!

Throwing his head from side to side in his struggles to
free himself, he caught sight of his naked body in the dressing table's mirror. Not only was he bound identically, but
he was in Madame Lucienne's bedroom.

And he was not alone!

Standing at the foot of the bed, looking as mean as all
hell, the Negro who had delivered the message from Marie
glowered at de Bracy with loathing.

To the prisoner's right, looking a mite pale but grimly
determined, was a tall young white man.

At the left of the bed, a slender, beautiful girl dressed in
unconventionally male attire opened and closed the jaws of
a pair of powerful pincers. With a shudder, de Bracy identified them as the identical implements used by the French-

man. They had been hurled aside and forgotten when he had stabbed Lucienne.

"He's awake, Belle," Darren remarked. "Can you understand me, de Bracy? Nod your head if you can."

"Take the gag out," Belle ordered, after the prisoner had given his assent to being able to understand. "Now he knows how Lucienne must have felt, we'll make a start."

"Our people are controling the street," Darren commented, crossing to look out of the window. "They're signaling that everything's clear and we don't need to worry about his screams being heard."

Watching the shock and fright displayed by de Bracy, Belle knew that they would make him answer their questions. That was the reason for bringing him to Madame Lucienne's room, where he had seen the woman tortured and would better recollect how she had suffered. Causing him to be stripped naked was a part of the process, as the conversation had been. Sweat poured down his face as Willie inserted the point of the Ames knife and severed the handkerchief gag.

"Wha-what do you want?" de Bracy demanded, trying to sound a whole lot braver than he felt.

"Information," Belle answered, clicking the jaws of the pincers in an anticipatory manner. "About Brunel, the Frenchman, and the Brotherhood for Southron Freedom."

"I—I don't know what you me—"

Before de Bracy could go further, cold steel was thrust against the inside of his right thigh. Even as he realized what was going to happen and tried to jerk his limb away, the pincers closed upon his flesh. Sudden, searing, numbing pain ripped into him. It was so shocking in its intensity that he could not as much as cry out in agony. In vain he tried to wrench himself free, but the ropes held him immobile.

After what had seemed like an eternity to the suffering man, although it was only a few seconds, the girl relaxed her hold.

"That's not true," Belle chided. "Lucienne was still alive when we found her, and she named you."

"I told the Frenchman to fin—" de Bracy began.

"Go on!" Belle ordered.

"You'll never make me talk!" de Bracy screeched. "So do your—agh!"

Again he felt the steel jaws take hold of him. This time it was closer to his groin, and the pain increased in severity. A moan of anguish burbled from his lips, and perspiration flooded from his pores until his whole body glistened with moisture.

"I wouldn't count on it," Belle drawled as she removed the pincers.

"I don't know, Belle," Darren put in, looking shaken but remembering his cue and prearranged speech. "They must have been sure we couldn't break him, or they wouldn't have let us know where he was."

"They expected us to kill him," Belle corrected. "Not to take him prisoner. The letter said that he was armed and a dead shot."

"Wha—how—what letter?" de Bracy gasped, drawing the required conclusions.

"The letter telling us where to find you," Darren explained. "Your good and loyal friends sold you out."

"The-they wouldn't!" the prisoner stated, but his voice lacked conviction.

"Who else could have told us where to find you?" Belle demanded. "*And* about Marie Larondel?"

That was the point which de Bracy had been considering ever since he had recovered. Apart from Brunel, the Frenchman, and the people with whom he had been hiding, his whereabouts had been a secret. Yet the Secret Service agents—he assumed correctly that was the status of his captors—had not only found him, but had known of a means by which to lure him from the safety of the house. Such information could only have come from another member of the Brotherhood.

"They even said that it was you who tortured and knifed Lucienne," Belle commented, watching de Bracy's every emotion. "That was to make sure we'd hate you enough to kill you on sight."

"That's what they wanted," Darren continued, while the prisoner showed increasing signs of anger and strain. "They knew we'd never rest until we caught whoever was responsible, so they decided to make you a sacrifice. After all, you'd brought all this trouble on them by killing—"

"I didn't kill her!" de Bracy screeched. "That was the Frenchman. He cut the maid's throat too."

"We'll need more than your word for that," Belle remarked. "Where is he, so that we can learn the truth?"

"He—he's left for Shreveport," de Bracy answered despondently. "But Brunel's in town. At the Hotel de Grace, calling himself 'Browning.'"

"And the Frenchman's gone to Shreveport?" Belle drawled, working the jaws of the pincers briskly.

"Ye-yes!" de Bracy yelled, fear of further torment causing him to struggle violently. "There's an important meeting there! It's true! I swear it's—"

Suddenly, in the heat of his tirade, the prisoner's face contorted and his body jerked as if in violent agony. His words ended in an incoherent gobble, and blood gushed from his mouth. Not only blood. A lump of flesh spat from between his lips and landed on the edge of the bed.

"Wha-what—" Darren gasped.

"Oh my God!" Belle exclaimed. "He's bitten through his tongue!"

# 14

# I JUST COULDN'T HOLD BACK

Everything was quiet and peaceful as Belle Boyd, Lieutenant St. Andre, and Willie entered the Hotel de Grace. A modestly priced establishment, it catered mainly for the family trade and people of a staid, sober nature. By twelve o'clock any night, the majority of its patrons were already in bed and the building silent.

Protesting that there "wasn't nobody about to let rooms," a Negro porter had opened the front door to St. Andre's knock. Studying the detective's badge of office—for he was not wearing uniform—the porter had allowed the party to enter. The reception desk had no attendant, so Belle crossed to it and obtained the required information from the register.

"Number thirteen," she told the handsome, smartly dressed young peace officer. "That's unlucky for somebody."

"Let's hope it ain't for none of us," Willie commented, fingering the hilt of Jim Bludso's Ames knife.

Knowing that there would be no hope of obtaining further information from de Bracy that night, if at all, Belle had decided not to waste time on him. She had left him in Darren and Willie's care, to be dressed and to be given such medical aid as they could manage, while she had gone out to make arrangements for his removal to a hospital. On her return, she had suggested that Darren continued to watch over de Bracy, leaving the arrest of Brunel to herself. It said much for the respect in which Darren now held the Rebel Spy that he had agreed—with one reservation. She must not make the attempt alone. Willie had insisted that he should accompany Belle. She had agreed but had declared that they must also have official backing.

Finding Lieutenant St. Andre at his bachelor apartment, after inquiring after him at Police Headquarters, Belle had been entirely frank about her activities of the night. She had been pleasantly surprised at his response to her story. Already aware of the gravity of the situation—and having known, respected, and liked Madame Lucienne for many years—he had merely commented that he hoped the Secret Service would not make a habit of such behavior in his jurisdictional area. Then he had asked how he could help his visitors.

General Handiman had ordered Belle and Darren to handle the affair without—if it was possible—allowing word of it to become known to the public. If it could be done, he wanted to end the Brotherhood for Southron Freedom quietly. That way, he would avoid presenting the South with martyrs and reminders of the past—or providing material which Northern radicals could use as propaganda against the ex-Confederate States.

Belle had requested that St. Andre alone of the police should accompany her and Willie to the Hotel de Grace. A very smart peace officer, the lieutenant had understood, and approved of, General Handiman's motives. So he had agreed to handle things as Belle had required.

"How do we take him?" Belle whispered, as they stopped at the door of Room Thirteen.

"Burst in and shove a gun against his head before he's fully awake," St. Andre suggested, drawing a Colt Peacemaker from under his jacket. "He won't open the door or give up without a fight if we give him the chance to do otherwise."

"Let me get rid of this skirt," Belle requested, unfastening the garment which she had donned before leaving Madame Lucienne's apartment. She stepped out of it, leaving her paletot jacket on. Then she drew the pick from its sheath and went on, "I may be able to open the lock."

Inserting the end of the pick, Belle felt it come into contact with an obstruction. She pushed gingerly, causing the key to move through the lock. It fell out and clinked softly as it hit the floor. Instantly Belle froze, alert for any hint that the sound had disturbed the man sleeping in the room. Nothing happened, and she assumed that the faint noise had been insufficient to waken Brunel. So she tested for and located the master lever.

"You'd make a good hotel thief," St. Andre praised sotto voce, as the lock clicked. "Now it's my turn."

Although she was wearing the gunbelt and the Dance rode in its low cavalry-twist draw holster, Belle did not argue the point. From the way he handled the Colt, St. Andre was more than competent in its use. So she stepped aside, leaving him unimpeded as he took her place at the door.

Cocking his Colt, St. Andre turned the handle. Flinging the door wide open, he sprang into the unilluminated room—and came *very* close to getting killed.

Always a light sleeper, Brunel had been even more so since his escape from the levee at the Baton Royale Glide. He had known that the Secret Service and the police were hunting for him, which had not tended to lend itself to a deep, untroubled slumber.

When the key had fallen, its collision with the floor had wakened him. He had not stirred, but his every faculty had been working to assess the danger. From the other faint noises, including the unmistakable "click-click-click" of a Colt's hammer being drawn to full cock, he had concluded that somebody was planning to enter his room. It might be no more than a thief, but Brunel felt disinclined to take the chance that it was anything so innocuous. Unlike de Bracy, he had not been misled by the lack of comment in the newspapers. The police and the Secret Service would be using every means available to them in an effort to trace him. Once they had found him, they would be unwilling to risk letting him escape or make a fight. Besides which, there was no reason why a thief would cock a gun at his door. If a robbery was planned, the thief would have tried a more easily accessible room and have held his weapon ready for use ever since entering the building.

Slipping the Starr Navy revolver from under his pillow, Brunel prepared to deal with the intruders. To his way of thinking, it was the ideal weapon for his purposes. Unlike the gun held by the intruder, the Starr had a double-action mechanism. It did not require cocking manually before it could fire: squeezing the trigger performed that function.

Raising the Starr, Brunel lined it along the bed, through the darkness, in the direction of the door. His right forefinger depressed the trigger gently, sensing the rearward movement of the hammer and halting it before reaching the point where it would be liberated to return to its original position.

Two things combined to save St. Andre that night.

On opening the door, the detective plunged through it at an angle which was calculated to carry him out of the line of fire if the suspect was ready for him. That alone would not have sufficed to keep him alive. As he prepared to enter, he had allowed the light from the passage's lamps to flood in ahead of him.

The sudden glare, coming on top of complete darkness, dazzled Brunel at exactly the right second. Involuntarily, and only slightly, he flinched just as he completed the withdrawal of the trigger. Down lashed the hammer to impact on the cylinder's uppermost percussion cap. A tiny spurt of flame passed into the powder charge in the chamber, and the gun roared. Muzzle-blast blazed brilliantly ahead of

Brunel, reducing his vision still further, but he heard a sharp cry of pain and knew that his lead had struck its mark.

Caught high in the left shoulder, with his left foot off the ground, St. Andre was spun around. Pain and shock caused him to yell out. Then he collided with Belle as she followed him.

Brunel had not been under the sheets, but was lying fully dressed on top of them. Swinging his feet sideways, he bounded off the bed to land facing the door. He squinted against the glare and could see well enough to lay his sights at the two figures on the threshold.

Entangled with the bewildered peace officer, Belle could not raise and use the Dance in an attempt to protect them. She felt herself and St. Andre shoved violently aside. Leaping by them, Willie hurled himself across the room. Staggering, Belle saw the light glinting on the blade of the Ames knife held low in the Negro's right hand. Then Brunel's revolver cracked. As its bullet did not come anywhere near her or strike another part of the room, Belle knew that Willie had been hit.

Twice more the Starr spat lead, but the .36-caliber bullets lacked the power to halt the charging Negro in his tracks. Around the upward licked the Ames knife with all the rage-induced strength of Willie's powerful body behind it. Brunel started to scream as the spear point found his lower belly. The sound ended in a strangled sob, for the blade had ripped his stomach open to the base of the breast-bone. Stumbling back against the wall, he went down with Willie following him. Again and again the Ames knife tore through flesh. Any one of the blows would have been fatal.

Slowly the Negro lurched to his feet. The knife was red with blood from point to guard, hanging loosely in his big right fist. As Belle darted towards him, he staggered and held himself upright against the wall.

"I—I'm real sorry, Miss Belle," Willie apologized weakly

as she supported him and helped him to the bed. "I just couldn't hold back when I saw him and recollected what he'd done to Massa Jim."

"That's all right, Willie," the girl replied. "You saved our lives. And a man like Brunel wouldn't have talked, no matter what we'd done to him. Lie back until I can get help for you."

"I—I reckon I killed that feller," Willie groaned, complying with her suggestion. "And you wanted 'special' to have him took alive."

"That's all right," Belle assured him gently. "I'm not sorry he's dead."

Which was true enough in one respect, Belle told herself. However, Brunel's death had deprived her of a means of learning what the Frenchman looked like. And he, of all the Brotherhood, was the man she wanted most badly to apprehend.

Voices rose and doors slammed as people, disturbed by the shooting, came from their rooms. Repeating her advice to Willie, Belle turned and went to join St. Andre. Holding his left hand to his wounded shoulder, the detective was telling the first of the awakened guests that he was a peace officer.

"Everything's under control," St. Andre went on. "But we need a doctor."

"I'm one!" announced a nightshirted, burly man. "Let me get my bag and I'll be right with you."

Heavy footsteps pounded on the stairs. Followed by a uniformed patrolman, General Handiman hurried along the passage.

"Darren got word to me that Brunel was here and you'd come after him," the General announced, seeing the surprise on Belle's face as he appeared in the doorway. Wanting to keep her presence a secret, if possible, he waved her to stay back beyond the range of vision of the onlookers in the passage. "Did you get him?"

"He's in here, by the wall," the girl replied. "Dead."

"You'd best put this on again," Handiman remarked, picking up the discarded skirt and handing it into the room. "Then keep out of sight until I can get rid of these people."

Showing brisk efficiency and considerable diplomacy, the General set to work at his self-appointed task. First he calmed the crowd, telling them that a notorious train and bank robber had been trailed to the hotel. The man had resisted arrest, so was shot down by the peace officers. Then Handiman apologized on behalf of the New Orleans Police Department for the hotel's guests having their sleep disturbed and requested that they should return to their rooms.

Something about the General's attitude, respectful, apologetic, yet warning that he would brook no interference, had caused the men and women to accede to his wishes. Before the doctor had returned, the passage was empty except for Handiman, the patrolman, and the manager. From the latter, the General had obtained permission to make use of an empty room on the same floor. Then, dismissing the man with further apologies, he had escorted Belle to it. So smoothly had he acted that not even the doctor had been granted a clear view of the girl.

"What happened?" Handiman asked, having lit the room's lamp and closed the door to ensure their privacy.

"We caught de Bracy, just as we planned, and made him talk. Then I came here with Lieutenant St. Andre and Willie. Either Brunel was suspicious and had stayed awake, or he was a light sleeper. Whichever it was, he shot St. Andre as we burst in and would maybe have killed us both if Willie hadn't tackled him. Willie was shot and hurt badly."

"The doctor will tend to him. Count on St. Andre to see to that. How much have you learned?"

"Not a lot. Only where to find Brunel. And that the Frenchman has left New Orleans. He's going to Shreveport. According to de Bracy, the Brotherhood for Southron Freedom is going to hold a special important meeting there. Of course, he may have been lying."

"Do *you* think he was?" Handiman wanted to know.

"He was a very frightened man," Belle replied. "And he spoke the truth about where we would find Brunel. If it was any other town but Shreveport, I'd be certain he hadn't lied."

"Why the doubts about Shreveport?"

*"You* know what's happening up there between the Army and the civilian population. With a man like that Colonel Szigo in command, it's not likely the Brotherhood would dare to make any public demonstration."

"Maybe they believe that would be the best town to make it in," Handiman suggested. "Lucienne told me they haven't been having any great or lasting success in stirring up the population so far. Oh, they pull in the usual rabble of malcontents and loafers. But the majority of the population don't see any sense in trying to secede again. There's not a lot of bitterness against the Union since Reconstruction has tailed off and folks are starting to get prosperous."

"So they want a town where there's real bitterness in which to make their grandstand play?" Belle drawled. "It's possible, but it could be as risky as all hell. Szigo would be only too pleased to put down a Rebel rebellion, if all I've heard of him is true."

"Well . . . " Handiman said, unwilling to make an open criticism of another serving officer.

"He's an embittered man," the girl elaborated. "Lieutenant Colonel is only his brevet rank. He knows that at any time he can be replaced with a substantive officer and be reduced to the rank and pay of captain. A man like that would leap at a chance to come to the attention of Washington, by *any* means. And there aren't so many means of doing it in the East. All the glory's being won out West."

"You seem to know plenty about Szigo," Handiman commented, neither confirming nor denying the statement. "Anyway, he's being replaced."

"Replaced?"

"We're not exactly deaf, blind, or stupid in Washington. Despite anything you agents in the field may believe, we do have some idea of what's going on around us. Like you, we've heard of what's happening in Shreveport, and a full colonel, Manderley I believe it will be, is being sent to relieve him. With orders to make peace with the civil population."

"I only hope that he arrives in time!" Belle declared fervently. "The Brotherhood has proved that they don't give a damn about shedding innocent blood. With those hundred Henry repeaters, they could raise hell around Shreveport, and it would spread all along the Red River—and beyond."

"You're right," Handiman conceded. "So in the morning I'm going to have all the people named by Lucienne visited and questioned."

"From what she said, few of them are deeply involved in the Brotherhood."

"That's why I'm only having them visited. I've found that people who go in for joining these impressively named clandestine organizations soon drop out again when they find it's not so secret after all."

"You might pick up a few details," Belle admitted, then looked at Handiman in a calculating manner. "You won't need me for it, will you, sir?"

"Have you something else in mind?"

"The Frenchman has gone to Shreveport—"

"And you want to go after him?"

"I intend to kill him," Belle stated calmly.

Studying the beautiful face as he listened to the flat, impersonal words, Handiman felt as if an icy hand had touched his spine. That had not been a mere empty figure of speech. The Rebel Spy meant to do exactly what she had said.

"He'll be among friends—" the General warned.

"That won't stop me."

"Some of them might be men you served with in the War—"

"Any friendship or loyalty I might have felt for them ended on the night of the *Prairie Belle,*" Belle answered. "General, I don't want my country ripped apart by another civil war. God! The last was bad enough. Next time, if it happens, it will be to a finish. They have to be stopped."

"I trust you, Colonel Boyd," Handiman assured her. "But the Frenchman—"

"He's caused the deaths of two good friends," Belle interrupted. "So I'm going to avenge them. And if I have to smash the Brotherhood to do it, so much the better for everybody's sake."

Again there was no bombast nor hysterical, unintended female threats—just a plain statement of facts.

Handiman found himself blessing the providence which had persuaded him to show good sense and hire Belle Boyd after the War had ended. With such a woman on their side, the Brotherhood for Southron Freedom would have been an even more terrible menace to the peace of the nation.

Yet, such was his faith in the Rebel Spy, the General—whose post as head of the Secret Service was not calculated to leave him with exaggerated faith in human nature and honesty—did not for a moment question her loyalty or doubt that she would remain true to the oath of allegiance she had sworn to the Union.

"Go to Shreveport," Handiman confirmed. "You have your identification documents?"

"In the secret pocket on my gunbelt," Belle replied.

"I'll give you letters of introduction to Manderley and Szigo, telling whichever's in command to give you every cooperation. You outrank Szigo, but my name will make sure that he appreciates that fact."

"Thank you, sir."

"Have you any plans for dealing with the situation?"

"None," Belle admitted. "I'll wait and see what develops. Or if it has developed, carry on from there. If I arrive before it happens, my uncle will do all he can to help me stop it. He's Colonel Alburgh Winslow."

"A sensible and influential man," Handiman praised. "In fact, he, his newspaper, and his group of moderate friends have done much to avert serious trouble between the Army and the townspeople."

"He'll keep right on doing it, come what may," Belle promised and glanced at the door as somebody knocked. "Shall I?"

"I will," Handiman corrected, opening up to admit St. Andre.

"It's only a flesh wound," the detective assured Belle when she had inquired about his injury. "But Willie's hurt bad. He's asking to see you, Belle."

"I'll go right away," Belle said, coming to her feet. "Is he alone?"

"The doctor's still with him, but he's an Army surgeon and won't talk," St. Andre replied. "My man's keeping the passage clear. By the way, I searched Brunel's belongings."

"Is there anything of interest?" Handiman asked.

"I found this sheet of paper in his wallet," St. Andre answered, producing and handing it over. "It may not mean anything. All it gives is a name. 'Sabot the Mysterious, last performance. Shreveport.' He's a really good magician, I've seen his perfor—"

"At Memphis they were going to hold a meeting in a theater," Belle interrupted. "How soon can I start for Shreveport?"

"The *Elegant Lady* leaves at dawn," St. Andre supplied the information. "You could ride her to Baton Rouge or Natchez and get another boat to Shreveport. There's pretty sure to be one waiting to make a connection with the *Lady*."

"That's what I'll do," Belle declared. "As soon as I've seen Willie, I'll go and gather my belongings. You'll see that Willie—"

"*I'll* attend to it, Miss Boyd," St. Andre promised. "He saved my life too."

"Miss Belle?" Willie groaned, as the girl went to his bed. "You's going to Shreveport after the Frenchman?"

"Yes, Willie," the girl agreed.

"Do me a lil favor."

"Anything."

"Take Massa Jim's ole Ames knife along," Willie requested, gesturing weakly to the weapon on the dressing table. "When you gets to where the ole *Belle* was sunk, throw it in so's he knows I done got that Brunel feller."

# 15
## YOU SHOULDN'T HAVE
## HIT HER

*Belle Boyd had carried out Willie's request on her way north along the Mississippi River and had arrived in Shreveport in time to witness the Brotherhood for Southron Freedom's special meeting. Unable to decide what lay behind the interruption to the final performance of Sabot the Mysterious, she was returning on foot to the theater with the intention of satisfying her curiosity.*

Feeling certain that his presence was not suspected by the "gal wearing pants," Hermy watched her disappear into an alley without any undue alarm. He saw nothing suspicious in her action. Shreveport had long since left behind the days when even an armed *man* could walk the streets without arousing curiosity. A girl dressed in such an unconventional manner would draw attention without the revolver hanging holstered on her right thigh. If she was headed to the theater for some clandestine purpose, she would wish to avoid being the source of interest or comment.

Reaching the mouth of the alley, Hermy could neither see nor hear the girl in its deeply shadowed length. So he hurried forward, wanting to know which way she had gone. At the rear end, he stepped cautiously out and looked in the direction she would have taken if she was going back to the theater. Still being unable to locate her, he scowled and wondered if he had been mistaken about having seen her entering the alley.

That question was answered promptly—although not in a manner he would have wished it to happen.

"To arms! To arms, in Dixie!" said a feminine voice from behind him.

Letting out a startled, profane expression, Hermy started to turn and sent his hand under his cloak-coat in search of a weapon.

Having detected Hermy following her, Belle had decided that she must throw him off her track. However, he might have been merely a casual, uninterested pedestrian and taking the same direction by coincidence. Or he could have been a peace officer, made suspicious by her male attire and the gunbelt. In either case, she had no desire to assault him.

Taking cover behind the corner of the building farthest from the theater, the girl had awaited developments. Everything had depended upon how the man reacted to her disappearance. Once she had seen that, she had settled upon her own line of action. It was simple, effective—and very much to the point.

The fact that the man had approached so cautiously had not been sufficient in itself to prove he belonged to the Brotherhood and had guessed her purpose. A peace officer following an armed suspect would have displayed a similar caution. However, Hermy's actions on arriving at the end of the alley had struck her as significant. When he had turned immediately to look in the direction which she would have taken on her way to the theater, she had been satisfied that he was following her on behalf of the organization.

Although Belle held her Dance, she did not use it as a firearm. To have done so would have made a noise and attracted unwanted interest in her actions.

Instead, the girl launched a savate attack with all the

power and precision she could muster. The area was so
dark that she could not make out details of the man's
clothing and appearance, other than that he was big
enough to be more than she could handle in a fight. So she
hoped to render him helpless without allowing him to defend himself.

Belle's boot drove upward between Hermy's spread-
apart thighs and caught him full in the groin with nauseat-
ing force. Unmentionable, unendurable agony ground its
way through his whole being. He started to fold over,
knees buckling and hands clutching at the stricken region.
His troubles had not yet ended.

The girl did not rely upon the kick to disable the man.
There was too much at stake for her to chance him recovering prematurely. So she swung the Dance. As it was an
open-frame revolver, like the 1860 Army Colt, she knew
better than to strike with the barrel. Instead she flung the
base of the butt savagely against the back of Hermy's close-
cropped skull. Down he went, like a steer under a
butcher's poleax.

Without waiting to establish the extent of her victim's
injuries, Belle holstered the Dance. She did not particularly care if the man was alive or dead. One thing she
knew. There was nothing more to fear from him at that
moment—nor for some time to come. Satisfied on that
score, she strode away in the direction the unconscious
man had been looking.

On drawing near the theater, following the back alleys,
Belle could see no traces of the evening's dramatic events.
Despite their enthusiastic response to the speech-making
and subsequent excitement, the crowd had not lingered in
the hope of further developments. Perhaps, once out in the
cool night air and removed from the symbols of their patri-
otic fervor, they had had second thoughts about their re-
awakened loyalty to the Confederate cause. Or they might
have scattered to spread the news of what had happened.

Belle hoped that it was the former contingency that had brought about the dispersal of the audience.

Whatever the reason, the building and its immediate surroundings were devoid of human life. That was just how Belle had hoped to find it. She noticed that half a dozen horses were standing fastened to the hitching rail behind the theater and decided that her return had been justified.

Keeping away from the animals, for she did not want them to raise an alarm at her presence, Belle passed along the dark alley by the theater. She was approaching the flight of stone steps which led up to the stage door when it opened.

Two long, silent strides carried Belle to the wall at the level side of the steps. There she crouched in the deep darkness, clear of the pool of light which was coming through the door. Heavy boots thudded close above her head, and men started to emerge from the theater.

"Vic!" called a voice which she recognized as that of Sabot the Mysterious, mingling with the sound of hurrying, lightly shod feet.

"What's wrong?" demanded the leading figure, bringing his companions to a halt.

Again Belle believed that she should know the voice, but failed to place it. Hoping for a clue, she remained in her position and stood as if turned to stone. Relying upon her dark clothing to help keep her concealed, she drew the Dance. Holding its white handle before her, she turned to face the wall. It was a trick she had learned from Big Sam Ysabel during the final hunt for Tollinger and Barmain.

"Selima's not in her dressing room," Sabot replied. "She's changed into her street clothes and's taken off."

"Where to?" growled the man Belle assumed to be "Vic."

"I'm damned if I know. Maybe back to the rooming house. But the way you laid into her when you came off the stage, she might have decided to run out on us. You shouldn't have hit her that way."

"So let the stupid whore go! She damned near gave the whole snap away, the way she carried on out there tonight. Damn it! She didn't even pretend to be worried when we came onto the stage."

"I warned you that she wasn't very smart," Sabot protested in a self-exculpatory tone.

"Can you trust her is more to the point," Vic stated.

"How do you mean?" the magician inquired.

"Would she inform on us?"

"I'm damned if I know what she'd do, pot-boiling mad like she was over you slapping her around. De Richelieu didn't help either, saying she deserved it and worse. She's a hot-tempered bitch at the best of times."

"God damn it!" Vic raged. "If I thought that she aimed to—"

"Somebody had best go and fetch her back," Sabot interrupted. "I can keep her under control. And I'll need her for the act when I reach Texas."

"Can't you train another girl?" Vic challenged. "One with a few brains this time."

"I could do that easily enough, if I could find the right kind of girl," the magician confirmed. "But leaving Selima behind won't make her feel any better disposed toward us. So she's got to be fetched back."

"What about the rest of our plans?" Vic asked.

"I'd say let them ride until we know what she's got in mind," Sabot counseled. "Get after her and bring her to me, then go on to Winslow's, is what I'd advise."

"You're right," Vic admitted grudgingly. "That's what we'll do."

"How about those two fellers who've gone to keep watch on him?" Sabot put in. "They're expecting you to get there soon."

"Matt's steady enough," Vic replied. "He'll stay put until we get there and stop that other bastard doing anything stupid. Once we've got her, or made sure she can't talk, we'll go ahead with the plan. What will you be doing?"

"Following de Richelieu's orders," Sabot replied coldly. "Heading for the river and the *Texarkana Belle*. If I've gone when you come back, send her after me, will you?"

"I'll do that," Vic promised. "We'd best not all go. Andy, you and Mick come with me, the rest stay on here."

A muttered rumble of agreement rose. Then some of the feet started moving. Three men came through the door and walked down the steps. Apparently Sabot did not want them to remain for long in view of the street. Almost as soon as they had emerged, he closed the door.

With the light blotted out and the darkness returned to the alley, Belle chanced looking over her shoulder. The men went by without noticing her crouching in the deepest shadows. However, the lack of light proved to be a mixed blessing. While the trio failed to locate her, she could not see any of their faces. All she managed to do was pick out certain significant details of their attire.

Something under six feet in height, with a good but not heavy build, the man in the lead—Belle assumed he was "Vic"—wore what could only be an Army kepi on his head. Given that much of a clue, she identified his outer garment as a cavalry officer's long cloak-coat—from beneath the hem of which thrust the scabbard of a saber that must be hanging on the slings of his waist belt. He had on regulation white gauntlets, she could see, and shining riding boots.

Taller than their companion or officer, the other two had on Burnside campaign hats, enlisted men's cloak-coats, and riding boots, although neither of them was armed with a saber.

Peering through the gloom, Belle watched the trio depart. The man she believed to be "Vic" seemed vaguely familiar. He strolled along with the cocky military swagger that was often the gait of an arrogant young officer. Trudging slightly to his rear, the other pair had the bearing of soldiers. They passed around the corner of the building.

Leather creaked soon after, and Belle heard the sound of horses moving away.

"Now what would soldiers be doing in there?" Belle mused as she retraced her steps along the alley. "Uncle Alburgh said that the town was off limits to them tonight."

Could Szigo have learned of the Brotherhood's visit and laid a trap for them at the theater?

That was not likely. Besides which, Szigo was no longer in command.

Why were the men, whoever they might be, so interested in her uncle that they had some of their number watching his home?

Then Belle remembered General Handiman's comment about Winslow and the other moderate, influential citizens —her uncle's companions at the theater that night, in fact —having prevented trouble between the civilian population and the soldiers.

"So that's the plan!" Belle gasped.

The three men had already ridden out of sight. Running to the horses which remained at the rail, Belle unfastened one's reins. She swung into the saddle, finding that it was of the military McClellan type. That proved little. Many such rigs were in civilian hands, being cheap and reasonably serviceable. Hoping that she would not be seen, she started the horse moving at a fast trot.

Traversing the town, Belle guided her borrowed mount along the darkened, almost deserted street towards Winslow's mansion. A big, bulky figure leaned against the gates to the property and peered in her direction. Then he turned and hurried into the garden. From his size and bulk, Belle knew that he was not one of her uncle's servants. In addition, she had noticed the shape of his hat and detected the glint of metal buttons on distinctive clothing.

There had been something furtive about his actions that was calculated to arouse her suspicions. Mainly, though, her interest had stemmed from the fact that he was an enlisted man of the United States Cavalry—or dressed like one.

Even as her mind was assimilating the details of the man's appearance and drawing conclusions from his presence, she rode by an empty buggy. It was parked unattended near the sidewalk before the commencement of Winslow's property. Glancing at it in passing, she noticed a civilian cloak lying on the seat.

A vehicle of that kind had passed shortly after she had caused her uncle's carriage to be halted. At the time, she had thought nothing of it other than to automatically make a note of its occupants' appearance. They had been a pair of big, burly, bareheaded men wearing either long overcoats or cloaks, despite the warmth of the evening.

The man who had followed her and had been left unconscious would have fitted that description!

Draping the one-piece reins on the horse's neck, Belle slid from the saddle without causing it to slow down from its walking gait. She could not see through the thick hedge which surrounded her uncle's garden, but felt that she might turn the lack of vision to her advantage. A gentle slap on the rump encouraged the horse to keep going. Winslow's stable would provide her with any further transportation she might require, and she was not concerned with where the animal went, now that it had served its purpose.

Allowing the horse to disappear along the street, Belle walked silently to the garden's gates and entered. There was no sign of the man, but a number of decorative bushes offered him a selection of hiding places. Giving no hint that she was aware of his presence, she strolled along the wide gravel path toward the front of the big, Colonial-style mansion.

Having no desire to be seen, and perhaps challenged, by the approaching rider, Matt had taken up his place of concealment behind a bush not far from the open gates. Vic's party would not arrive singly, so the rider could not be one of the Brotherhood. One disadvantage to the cover he had selected was that he could not see the street. However, he had no difficulty in hearing the horse's hoofbeats and knew that it was going straight by.

On the point of emerging, Matt saw a slender, boyish figure walking through the gates. At first he felt puzzled, wondering why the newcomer would be visiting Winslow at such a late hour. Then realization came with the impact of a kick in the stomach.

That was no boy, but a slim girl wearing male clothing!

Matt recollected how Hermy had claimed to have seen a "gal wearing pants" emerge from Winslow's carriage. At the time, Matt had been suspicious of his companion's veracity. He had believed that Hermy was lying, as an excuse to quit the potentially dangerous business upon which they were engaged. So he had accepted Hermy's story and given the order for "her" to be followed. He had not expected to see his companion again and had felt that it was good riddance.

From all appearances, Hermy had been telling the truth. That he should have mentioned a girl wearing riding breeches and for one to turn up at Winslow's house went beyond the bounds of pure coincidence. Hermy had seen the girl, but she must have eluded him in some way. That would not have been a difficult task in Matt's opinion. He had formed a very low impression of his companion's intelligence and abilities.

Well, the man concluded as he crept from behind the bush, she would find Matt Cilstow a much more difficult proposition than the dull-witted Hermy.

Moving cautiously across Winslow's well-barbered lawn, Matt kept to his victim's rear as he converged with her. He realized that his progress would be anything but noiseless once he set foot upon the gravel of the path. So he intended to get as close as possible before doing it.

One thing was in Matt's favor, or so he told himself. The girl was unaware of his presence.

With that thought in mind, Matt stepped onto the path. He had gauged his distance perfectly. Before the girl could take fright from hearing his footsteps and turn or try to draw her revolver, he was close enough to make his move. Encircling her from the rear with his brawny arms, he pinioned her elbows against her sides. He intended to crush her savagely, driving the air from her lungs and rendering her incapable of crying for help. Having taken that precaution, he would fling her down so that she could be completely subdued. Then, carried away to some secluded spot, she could be induced to answer questions.

All of which might have worked, but for one small, yet vitally significant detail. Belle was far from being as unsuspecting of her peril as Matt had fondly imagined. Moreover, by using some of the techniques which she had learned from Dusty Fog to augment her savate, she had hopes which ran parallel to her assailant's intentions.

Instead of trying to pull away, as Matt expected and was ready to prevent, Belle seemed to wilt in his grasp. She also contracted her torso as far as possible and hugged inward with her trapped arms. Having decided how she would react, the man was disconcerted by her refusal to behave in the expected manner.

Clenching her left fist, Belle ground its knuckles vigorously against the back of Matt's right hand. At the same time, she stamped the heel of her right foot against the edge of his left instep. The double pangs of pain caused him to separate his hands before the fingers interlocked. Instantly Belle rammed her rump into him, gaining a little more room to maneuver. Bending at the waist, she reached between her legs in an attempt to catch hold of his left ankle.

At which point, her counter started to go wrong.

Before she could lay hands on his leg—with the intention of jerking it upward, sitting on his knee, and toppling him backward with considerable force—Matt's hands had clamped onto her shoulders and snatched her upright.

"Smart whore, huh?" the man gritted, moving his fingers until they coiled about her throat and his thumbs pressed forward on the nape of her neck. "Well, I'm too smart for you."

Already Belle had commenced a line of action calculated to refute Matt's claim to possessing greater intelligence. Once again, she failed to respond in the way her attacker had anticipated.

Despite the crushing, choking pressure being exerted upon her windpipe, Belle did not attempt to tear her neck free by brute force. To do so against her captor's strength would have been futile. Instead, she tilted her torso toward him. Her right leg raised and bent, then flung back its foot to spike the heel hard on to his right kneecap.

Matt let out a sharp intake of breath and relaxed his pressure a trifle. Instantly Belle's hands whipped up and over her head to grab his thick wrists. Using her left foot as a pivot, she swiveled her body sharply to the right. Snatching the man's loosened fingers from her neck, she elevated his left arm and jerked his right underneath it. Swiftly forcing his left elbow on to the right arm, she invested all her weight and strength into a forward and downward thrusting heave. Thrown off balance, Matt's feet rose into the air. His Burnside hat tumbled off as he sailed over in a near perfect somersault.

Too near, in fact!

Belle released her hold once she had got him into the air. Staggering with the force she had put into the effort, she saw that he had contrived to land on his feet instead of alighting hard on the base of his spine. However, he stumbled and seemed to be in danger of falling flat on his face.

Wanting to incapacitate her assailant, Belle fought to regain her equilibrium. Doing so took her four running strides. In control of her movements, she swung around and darted in his direction. Too late she observed that he too had recovered from the effects of the throw.

Obligingly, if inadvertently, Belle ran into range. Swinging toward her, Matt whipped his left arm up and across. The back of his hand collided with her cheek. Bright lights burst in front of her eyes. Gasping in pain and half-blinded by the tears it caused, she went spinning helplessly across the path. Catching her left toe against her right ankle as she reached the lawn, she tripped. Her horse-riding instincts helped her to soften the impact of the fall. For all that, she landed hard and rolled over three times before coming to a halt, supine, dazed, and winded, on the grass.

Spitting out threats of violence, Matt thumbed open his holster and started to draw his revolver. He had decided against trying to take that hellcat a prisoner and intended to close her mouth permanently.

Belle saw what the man planned to do but was too befuddled to make a move in her own defense. Out came the revolver, slanting in her direction. A shot rang out; but it was the flat crack of a rifle and from farther away than her attacker's weapon. With the top of his head seeming to erupt like a burst sack of flour, the man was flung sideways and to the ground.

Lights showed at the doors of the mansion. Grasping a rifle, Winslow sprinted along the path, followed by Hector carrying a lantern.

"Are you all right, Belle?" Winslow demanded.

"I've felt better," the girl admitted. "But it could have been worse. How did you—"

"I've been watching him hanging about at the gate ever since Hector said that he'd followed us home," Winslow explained. "When he attacked you, I got my Winchester lined and stopped him as soon as you were out of my line of fire. He's a soldier!"

"It looks that way," Belle admitted, standing up and approaching the body. "Bring the light here, please, Hector."

Bending closer, Belle studied the buttons on the blue jacket. At first glance, they looked like the standard issue. There were, however two noticeable differences. Each button had the usual spread eagle and three-pointed shield insignia, but instead of the "A," "C," or "I" by which the wearer's branch of service—Artillery, Cavalry, or Infantry —was revealed, it bore the letter "D." And while ordinary buttons displayed no further adornment, the ones worn by her attacker carried an inscription.

*"Ad Astra Per Aspera,"* Belle read out.

"That's the state motto of Kansas," Winslow interpreted. "And the 'D' means 'Dragoon.' He must have belonged to some Kansan militia outfit and kept the buttons on his jacket."

"I don't think he served in the Blue," Belle contradicted. "Can you have two horses saddled, Uncle Alburgh? You and I have to go out. Pray God we're in time. If we're not, there'll be murder done tonight, and we'll be on our way to another civil war come morning."

# 16

## SHE'S DONE FOR, VIC!

Although the sergeant of the guard looked with a hint of incredulity from Belle to the identification card she had shown him and back again, he did not attempt to question the validity of the document.

"You want me to send a man with you, ma—col—ma—" the noncom inquired, uncertain of how he should address the visitor.

"Is that Headquarters?" Belle asked, indicating the large, well-lit mansion ahead of her.

"Yes'm," the sergeant confirmed. "You'll find the colonel up on the first floor, in the officers' club. I'll have a man—"

"I can find it," Belle assured him, and started her horse moving.

"You reckon that paper she showed us's real, sarge?" the sentry wanted to know as Belle rode away.

"I dunno," admitted the noncom. "What I *do* know is that, happen it is for real, I didn't want to stop her. That gal's not like the other. She's a lady. And talking of Selima, where the hell's Brody?"

"Maybe the new colonel's got him up there in officers' country for a drink 'n' a talk, friendly-like," grinned the

sentry. "This here's a no good chore, sarge. There's too
many folk coming tonight."

"It's to be expected," commented the sergeant. "With
the change of command and all."

If Belle had heard the reference to Selima, she might
have been very interested. As it was, she rode the mount
borrowed from her uncle toward the hitching rail by the
porch of the mansion.

Having explained her theory to Winslow, Belle had left
him to take care of certain precautions. Then she had
mounted the horse which he had selected and set off for
the Army post. She prayed that she might be in time to set
the soldiers into motion. Given luck, anyway, she had
spoiled the devilish scheme which the Brotherhood for
Southron Freedom had planned to implement in Shreveport.

Leaving her horse alongside two others which were teth-
ered to the hitching rail, Belle slipped off the cloak which
she had donned at Winslow's house. She had worn the
garment to avoid attracting attention during the ride to the
post, but the night was too warm for it to be comfortable.
So she draped it over her saddle, secured the horse, and
ascended the steps to the porch. Crossing it, she tried the
front doors. They opened, and she stepped into the dimly
illuminated main hall.

Hearing Belle enter, a man turned from where he had
been standing at the door of one of the rooms which led
from the hall. Stiffening slightly, he threw a glance at the
door. Then he walked toward the girl. He advanced with a
somewhat arrogant gait. His whole bearing hinted that he
belonged in the building but that he doubted whether the
newcomer did.

Something about the man caught Belle's eye and started
thoughts leaping in her head. Under six feet in height, he
had a sturdy, yet not exceptional build and a handsome,
but hard face. An officer's kepi sat at a rakish angle on his
head, and his uniform was that of a cavalry captain. Going

by his white gauntlets and the saber dangling from the slings of his weapon belt—balanced by the holster at his right side—he was performing some military duty rather than relaxing after a day's work.

The duty could not be officer of the day, Belle realized. That was the province of first or second lieutenants, not captains.

"Good evening," the officer greeted, with coldly polite formality, while still some distance from the girl. "Can I help you?"

Was he speaking louder than necessary? Belle mused. Or did he always adopt that carrying tone of voice?

Even as she pondered on those points, Belle realized that the captain had spoken with more than a hint of a Southron accent. What was more, she felt sure that she had heard a similar style of speaking already that night. She observed that he was starting to draw off his right gauntlet—

And the flap of his holster was open!

Taken at its face value, the latter was not an important detail. Considering the other items which Belle had noticed, it might be highly significant.

There were Southrons serving as officers in the United States Army—men who had felt that their loyalties lay in preserving the Union or who had been disenchanted with the Confederate States' way of life. So the accent was not out of place.

However, Belle's study of the captain had led her to class him as a bow-necked, parade ground martinet who would take great pride in his personal appearance. Such a man would only allow the flap of his holster to be unfastened if he was expecting to need the revolver it carried. There could be no such need or expectancy at the Headquarters building of an Army post, unless . . .

Thinking back to her second visit to the theater, Belle remembered the conversation she had overheard between Sabot the Mysterious and the man he had called "Vic." It had had to do with the possibility of the magician's assistant informing the authorities of their activities. "Vic" had promised to find her. What was more, he had been wearing the uniform of an officer in the United States Cavalry. The cloak-coat and the darkness had combined to prevent her from discovering his rank, but she had seen the saber he was wearing.

At the time, Belle had been puzzled by seeing the weapon. In most cases, a saber merely served as a symbol of authority when performing some duty.

A duty like arresting men guilty of treason!

That would be a task assigned to a captain!

Before Belle could take her thoughts any further, somebody opened the door at which the captain had been standing. A tall, burly corporal stepped out in a furtive manner. Raw scratches showed on his cheeks and hands, as if he had been raked by a cat's claws . . .

Except that the bloody furrows were spaced at wider intervals than any domestic cat's talons would spread.

"She's done for, Vic," the corporal said as he appeared. "Lord, did she—"

On hearing the words, a hot flush of anger played over the officer's features. He saw a flicker of understanding cross the girl's face and sensed that, somehow or other, she realized he had no right to be in the building. If so, his "corporal's" stupidly incautious words would have been proof for her that something was radically wrong.

There was only one thing for "Vic" to do.

Snapping his right hand back to the already unfastened holster, the captain started to draw his revolver. The move was made with some speed and hinted that he was well used to the kind of rig in which the United States Army insisted that its personnel carry their side arms.

Everything was suddenly plain to Belle. By some trick of acoustics, Vic's voice had been distorted at the theater. So she had failed to recognize it when he had addressed her on her arrival. Yet she now realized why it had sounded vaguely familiar. The first time she had heard it was on the stage of the theater. Unless she was badly mistaken, "Vic" had been the second of the spokesmen.

Pure instinct caused the girl to respond to the menace. Already her right hand had turned and was wrapping its fingers about the smooth ivory grips of the Dance. Throwing herself sideways, she swept the gun from leather. Its hammer went back under her thumb, and she swung the barrel into alignment as she had done so many times in practice.

Even as Vic's revolver cleared the cumbersome holster's lip, flame licked from the barrel of Belle's Dance. Aimed by instinctive alignment, the .36 ball ploughed into "Vic's" forehead. Releasing his revolver unfired, the captain pivoted almost gracefully and sprawled headlong to the floor.

Realizing that he had made a mistake, the corporal was equally aware of the danger to himself. He saw his companion shot down and was all too aware of the slender girl's skill in handling her gun. It was a standard of ability to which he could not aspire. So he did not make any attempt to do so. Jumping back into the room, he jerked the door closed behind him.

Darting across the hall, ignoring the shouts which rang out from the floor above, Belle heard the man's feet crossing the room. Then glass shattered and the footsteps faded away. Belle knew what the sound implied. So she did not offer to enter the room. Turning, she ran along the passage to the front door.

Starting to go through, the girl discovered that the man had moved swiftly after leaping through the window of the room. He had also taken the opportunity to arm himself— a fact of which Belle was rapidly made aware.

Having sprinted to the front of the building, the corporal had been on the point of freeing his horse when he had heard Belle approaching the front entrance. He also heard the sentry yelling for the sergeant of the guard, but treated it as of secondary importance. That blasted girl not only dressed like a man, she could shoot like one. So she was a greater potential danger than the soldiers of the guard. They might hesitate before opening fire upon a man they took to be a corporal. At least, they would most likely delay for long enough to let him ride them down and burst through the gates to safety.

First, however, the girl must be dealt with.

Thrusting forward his Army Colt, the corporal snapped off a shot in Belle's direction. He fired fast and without making sure of his aim—never a combination conducive to accuracy.

Lead impacted on the frame of the door in front of the Rebel Spy. Jerking back involuntarily, she paused to review the situation. Hearing sounds which told her the man was mounting his horse, she made her second attempt to effect an exit. Going through the door in a rolling dive, she halted on her left side at the edge of the porch. Clasping the Dance's butt in both hands, she looked swiftly along the barrel at the corporal's rage-distorted face.

Then Belle changed her point of aim. A living, if wounded, prisoner could satisfy her curiosity on a number of points. Chiefly, given the correct inducements, he could describe the Frenchman and instruct Belle on the source of her hatred.

So the girl lowered the Dance's barrel until it pointed at the corporal's right shoulder. Controlling his restless horse, he was trying to bear down on her. She refused to let that fluster her or change her intention.

The Dance barked, but Belle believed that she had heard a second, more distant detonation. Aimed truly, her bullet entered the blue jacket in an ideal position to break his clavicle. The light load of a Navy-caliber* revolver

---

* The Navy had not selected the caliber of .36 because—as many soldiers boasted—it was easier to kill a sailor than a soldier. A revolver of that caliber could be made light enough—two pounds, ten ounces in the Colt Navy Model of 1851, as opposed to the four pounds, one ounce weight of the same

might lack stopping power, as had been proven when Brunel had shot Willie, but Belle was confident that the corporal could not ride far while suffering from such an injury.

As Belle's bullet found its mark and entered, something burst violently out of the corporal's chest in a spray of blood, splintered bones, and pulverized flesh. His body jerked uncontrollably, and blood gushed from a far vaster wound than the Navy's ball could have made. Shying violently, his horse flung him from the saddle. Falling onto the mount "Vic" had used, he was pitched from its rump and to the ground.

Coming to her feet, Belle sprang from the porch. While approaching the writhing shape, she saw the sergeant turning and addressing the sentry. The latter lowered his smoking carbine and attempted to offer some explanation. Ignoring him, the sergeant urged the remainder of the guard to increase their speed and led them on the double toward the house.

Although Belle held her Dance ready for use, she saw that she would not require it. Before she reached the stricken corporal, his body gave a final convulsive shudder and went limp. Lowering the hammer to rest on the safety notch between two of the percussion caps, she returned the Dance to its holster. Without considering how the action might be interpreted, she turned to go back into the mansion.

The sergeant of the guard did not know what had happened inside the building, having only the evidence of his eyes to go on. What he could see looked highly suspicious and dangerous to his rank. A long-serving soldier, he was inclined to take the side of the shot "corporal" for want of better evidence. If the sentry—who had fired without or-

---

*Company's Model 1848 Dragon—for a man who would be on foot and indulging in strenuous activities to spend long periods wearing it holstered at his belt. The .44 "Army" caliber handguns had been intended primarily for use by Dragoons and other mounted men.*

ders—had killed another member of the U.S. Cavalry, the sergeant would be held responsible. So he intended to hold on to the only witness, who might also be a guilty party.

"Hold it right there, lady!" the sergeant bellowed, making the command in such a manner that she could not use it against him if the rank on her identification card should be genuine.

Wisely, Belle complied. She guessed that the sergeant had reached an erroneous conclusion regarding her actions. Although the corporal's horse had bolted on being relieved of his weight, two more animals were fighting their reins at the hitching rail. So the noncom suspected that she could be contemplating mounting one and making a dash for safety.

The arrival of the guard, glowering suspiciously in the light of the lanterns two of them carried, coincided with the appearance of three officers at the front door.

"What's happening?" demanded the burly, bearded colonel in the lead.

"I'm damned if I know, sir," the sergeant of the guard admitted. "That two-bar come running like his ass was on fire just after we heard a window busted. He jumped on his hoss, then this ga—lady come out shooting."

"He'd shot at her first," protested the sentry, wishing to absolve himself of blame for his spontaneous action. "And was set to do it again."

"That's right, sir. He did," conceded the noncom. He was still uncertain of Belle's standing in the affair and aimed to take no chances.

"Who is this man?" asked the major, who had been last of the trio to emerge, studying the dead "corporal" in the light of the lanterns. "I don't seem to recognize him."

"He come in with the captain's'd brought the dispatches for Colonel Szigo, sir," the sergeant explained.

"Dispatches?" grunted the lanky, miserable lieutenant colonel, making his first comment. *"Dispatches?* I've seen no damned captain—"

"But he came maybe ten minutes back, sir," the sergeant protested. "He said I didn't need to send nobody with him, 'cause him and the corporal knew their way. Then the sentry told me the gal was coming, and they rode up here while I was turning to look."

"Which girl?" asked Colonel Manderley, and indicated Belle. "This one?"

"No, sir," corrected the noncom. "It was Selima, that magical feller's gal. She come asking to see Colonel Szigo. Wouldn't say what she wanted, 'cepting that it was important. Looked like she'd been getting slapped around by somebody, and she was madder'n a boiled owl. So I told Brody to fetch her up here."

"She never arrived either," the major growled. "Just what the hell is going on here?"

"I think I can explain," Belle put in. "But you'd better have somebody look in that open room along the hall first. You'll find the girl in there, and your soldier. I hope that he's still alive, but I'm sure she isn't."

"Do it, Major!" Manderley ordered, eyeing Belle with interest and appraisal. After the officer had departed, he went on, "I think explanations are in order, young lady."

"Shall we go inside?" the girl suggested. "I would prefer to talk in private, if that's all right with you."

"Come with me, please," Manderley consented. "Sergeant, leave the body until the officer of the day comes and searches it."

Clearly the major had not wasted a second in carrying out his orders. As Manderley and Szigo followed Belle into the hall, he appeared at the door of the room. Other officers were gathered and one was kneeling alongside "Vic's" body.

"There's a dead girl in here," the major declared. "She's been strangled. Brody's here, too, unconscious. Get inside and do what you can, Doctor."

"Excuse me, sir," said the officer, rising from his examination of "Vic." "I know this man. But he shouldn't be wearing that uniform."

"How do you mean?" Szigo demanded irritably.

"His name is Victor Brandt, sir," the officer elaborated. "He was a lieutenant in the Fourth Cavalry when I was with them. But he was busted out of the Army when some soft-shell* politicians reported that he was abusing and mistreating the enlisted men."

Until she heard the "captain's" name, Belle had wondered if he might be the Frenchman. She had felt sure that he was the second of the spokesmen—which had suggested that he was a senior member of the Brotherhood. When he had spoken to Sabot at the stage door, it had been in hard, imperious tones that might have been indicative of a hasty temper. From the conversation, it had been he who punished Selima for her unsatisfactory behavior on the stage.

Against that, Belle had heard another name mentioned. "De Richelieu" was definitely of French origin. Its owner had clearly approved of "Vic"'s chastisement of Selima, implying that he had been the first spokesman. He might also have been the Frenchman and had held back from dealing with the girl because he had known that he could not hold his temper within reasonable bounds.

"Victor Brandt" was certainly not a French name. Nor did it seem likely that a man with the Frenchman's warped pleasure in inflicting pain would have left the disposal of a traitress to another member of the Brotherhood. So Belle decided that her quest had not yet ended. She would have to seek elsewhere before she could avenge the deaths of Madame Lucienne and Jim Bludso.

---

* *Soft-shell: a crusading liberal-intellectual.*

# 17

# I'M NOT SORRY SABOT ESCAPED

"They've all got clean away, Miss Boyd," Colonel Manderley announced grimly as the girl entered his office at one-thirty in the morning. "My men raided the theater, but it was deserted. By that time, the *Texarkana Belle* had left and they didn't even get Sabot."

"How about my uncle and his friends?" Belle demanded anxiously.

"They're safe. If the thing was planned as you suspected, they didn't carry it out. Probably because Brandt wasn't there to lead the others."

"Yes. They're weren't likely to have two 'officers.' Your men didn't locate the arms, I suppose?"

"Not yet. I've got them scouring the woods around the city. It's possible the Brotherhood has them hidden somewhere in Shreveport, I suppose."

"I doubt that," Belle objected. "It's my belief that they wouldn't want to take a chance on losing their weapons. So they'll have held them somewhere that would allow them to be moved to safety if anything went wrong. Either out in the woods or along the river."

"That's how I see it," Manderley admitted. "I hope we do find them. A hundred repeaters, even old Henrys, in the hands of men like the Brotherhood isn't something I care to contemplate."

Having invited Belle to accompany him and Szigo into his office, Manderley had checked her documents. He had read Handiman's letter of introduction, then asked the girl how he might best be able to help her. Making her suggestions, she had told the officers about the Brotherhood's activities. Szigo had not been pleased to learn that he had been duped, but he had been wise enough to keep his opinions to himself.

Although much of Belle's summation had been speculative, she had come close to the truth in her explanation of the night's events.

Having stirred up considerable ill-feeling against the Union among the audience at the free show, the Brotherhood had planned to keep tempers at the boiling point. If their next move had worked, it would have probably resulted in open conflict between the citizens and the soldiers.

Disguised as members of the United States Army in uniforms taken from the Dragoons' equipment bales, Brandt's party was to have "arrested" Winslow and his companions for their part in the treasonable activities at the theater. With them all collected, they would have been murdered. Not only would their deaths—apparently at the hands of men under Szigo's command—have inflamed the townspeople with a desire for revenge, it would have removed the restraining influence which Winslow and the others might have exerted.

A man like Szigo could have been relied upon to add further fuel to the fires of hatred by his attitude. Probably he would have refused to even investigate the accusations. Faced with what he would have been only too pleased to call an open rebellion, he would strike back. There would have been fighting, with Southrons and soldiers killed.

Such an incident could not have been kept out of the newspapers. Once the story got out, it would spread like a brushfire. Agitators in both the North and the South would pounce on it. Perhaps it would not lead immediately to a second secession, but the seeds would have been sown. The Brotherhood would have made sure that they developed and blossomed into an open break from the Union.

The plan had started to go wrong when Brandt had punished Selima. Bitter at the treatment, she had been determined to take her revenge. Leaving the theater, she had visited the rooming house in which she was boarding. After collecting her portable belongings, she had set out to lay her information. That had presented her with a problem. She wanted to benefit financially from her treachery and had wondered who might best suit her needs. Knowing little about the Brotherhood, other than that its members claimed to be well supported in their activities, she had decided against consulting the local civilian authorities. They might have been in league with her employers. So she had elected to take her news to the Army. She had known Szigo and other officers, which would ensure that they granted her an interview.

What the girl had not known was that her departure had been discovered. Brandt and the two soldiers had gone to the rooming house and learned that she had already left. Guessing which way she would go, Brandt had sent Mick to the theater with orders not to start the plan until he returned. Then he and Andy had made for the post, hoping to find her before she arrived. Missing her, due to taking a more direct route, they had been interviewing the sergeant of the guard when they had seen her coming. So they had made their way to the Headquarters building and lain in wait for her. Her arrival with an escort had presented no problems. Brody had been clubbed insensible as he entered, and the girl silenced. At Brandt's suggestion, Andy had taken Selima into the room and dealt with her. A "captain," even one who was not a regular member of the garrison, would have been less likely to have his presence in the building questioned. So he had left the silencing to his companion while he kept watch.

When Brandt had not returned, Sabot the Mysterious had taken it upon himself to cancel the rest of the plan. Dismissing the men and sending a warning to de Richelieu, who was waiting with the arms at a farm five miles from Shreveport, the magician had made his departure as planned on the *Texarkana Belle*. Assuming that the horse which Belle had taken had pulled free its reins and wandered off, the conspirators had attached no greater significance to its disappearance. Most of them, indeed, had been so eager to make good their escapes that they had not given the matter a second thought. Before the Army had commenced its search, the members of the Brotherhood for Southron Freedom were well on their way to safety.

While being very eager to capture the agitators, Manderley had also been aware of how delicate the situation was. He had approved of Szigo's decision to place the town off limits that night, so he did not want to alarm the population—or permit accusations of failure to keep his word—by sending a large armed force in search of the Brotherhood. Compromising, he had sent a dozen picked men under the command of his most trustworthy officer— a major who had never approved of Szigo's handling of the civilian population. Reinforcements had stood to arms, ready to follow the patrol if there should have been any shooting. The major had returned from his abortive mission and reported to Manderley. Having sent to the room where Belle was catching some badly needed sleep, the colonel had brought her up to date with the events of the night.

"We found that feller you told us about," Manderley went on. "He was still unconscious, and the doctor says his skull is fractured. So he might not remember anything when, or if, he recovers. That must have been a hell of a crack you gave him."

"It seemed like a good thing to do at the time," Belle answered. "I hope that he can talk though."

"Yes. It might help us to locate the others," Manderley growled. "Damn it, ma—Colonel Boyd, if you'd—"

"I've been thinking the same thing, Colonel," the girl answered, without sounding apologetic. "But I acted as I thought best at the time. Everything at the theater pointed to Sabot being in cahoots with the intruders. It was too much of a coincidence that he would have selected a trick that fitted their requirements so perfectly. To say nothing of it being highly unlikely that they could have substituted their portraits for whatever he had hidden behind the curtain. Then there had been Selima's behavior. She acted as if nothing was wrong. It caused her death in the end, poor little fool. On top of it all, the orchestra had been ready to play 'Dixie' at just the right moment."

"None of which would have been remembered, or considered, if they'd succeeded in their plan," Manderley admitted.

"It wouldn't," Belle agreed. "I went back to the theater to see if there was any way I could prove what I suspected. Then, when I realized what they must be planning, I had to warn Uncle Alburgh and his friends. He sent word to them, and I came here as quickly as I could."

"I'm not blaming you, Colonel," Manderley stated. "There's few enough would have realized what was being planned."

"Thank you, sir. Do you think that your men will find the arms?"

"It's not likely. The Brotherhood must have become suspicious when Brandt didn't return. If so, they won't have lingered in this neck of the woods. If I make too big a fuss searching for them, it's going to arouse a lot of comment. The truth about what's happened could get out, and neither of us wants *that*."

"Nor do our superiors," Belle commented wryly. "We're safe as far as the civilian population is concerned. Uncle

Alburgh will have his newspaper pass off the business at the theater as a stupid, ill-advised, but unimportant piece of foolishness. Handled that way, people will have forgotten it by the end of the week. But not if the truth gets out. Yankee radicals will make a big thing of it, and the Brotherhood will suggest that the Army really intended to arrest and murder Uncle Alburgh as an example to other Southrons not to attend treasonable assemblies."

"You're right," Manderley conceded.

"I'm not sorry Sabot escaped," Belle remarked.

"Why not?"

"Aren't there two Navy steam launches here in Shreveport?"

"Yes. They come under my command and are used for policing the river."

"One of them could easily take me to Mooringsport," Belle said thoughtfully.

"Not before the *Texarkana Belle* arrives," Manderley warned. "I had thought of sending one of them after her to arrest Sabot."

"I'm pleased that you didn't," Belle drawled. "With luck, and a little planning, he's going to take me to the rest of the Brotherhood—and the Frenchman."

How Belle Boyd followed the Brotherhood for Southron Freedom in search of the Frenchman is told in *The South Will Rise Again*.

# J.T. EDSON

## Brings to Life the Fierce and Often Bloody Struggles of the Untamed West

| | | |
|---|---|---|
| __ THE BAD BUNCH | 20764-9 | $3.50 |
| __ THE FASTEST GUN IN TEXAS | 20818-1 | $3.50 |
| __ NO FINGER ON THE TRIGGER | 20749-5 | $3.50 |
| __ SLIP GUN | 20772-X | $3.50 |
| __ A MATTER OF HONOR | 20936-6 | $3.50 |
| __ BLOODY BORDER | 21031-3 | $3.50 |
| __ ALVIN FOG, TEXAS RANGER | 21034-8 | $3.50 |
| __ OLE DEVIL AT SAN JACINTO | 21040-2 | $3.50 |
| __ HELL IN PALO DURO | 21037-2 | $3.99 |
| __ OLE DEVIL AND THE MULE TRAIN | 21036-4 | $3.50 |
| __ VIRIDIAN'S TRAIL | 21039-9 | $3.99 |
| __ OLE DEVIL AND THE CAPLOCKS | 21042-9 | $3.99 |
| __ TO ARMS! TO ARMS IN DIXIE! | 21043-7 | $3.99 |

### FLOATING OUTFIT SERIES

| | | |
|---|---|---|
| __ GO BACK TO HELL | 21033-X | $3.50 |